DOCTOR WHO
GHOST LIGHT

based on the BBC television series by Marc Platt
by arrangement with BBC Books, a division of BBC
Enterprises Ltd

MARC PLATT

Number 149 in the
Target Doctor Who Library

A TARGET BOOK
published by
the Paperback Division of
W H Allen & Co Plc

For
Ian, Margaret and the wonderful Alice

A Target Book
Published in 1990
By the Paperback Division of
W H Allen & Co Plc
338 Ladbroke Grove, London W10 5AH

The BBC producer of *Ghost Light* was John Nathan-
Turner
The director was Alan Wareing
The role of the Doctor was played by Sylvester McCoy

Printed and bound in Great Britain by
Cox & Wyman Ltd, Reading

ISBN 0 426 20351 8

Contents

1

Tropic of Perivale

It was hot, the dog days of August. The girl ran along the footpath, her straggly hair flying and a dust storm rising behind her. She nearly collided with a woman who was walking a baby in a push-chair, but she careered on and spun round a corner. Flinging herself through a gap in the scrubby bushes, she came to rest at the foot of an old brick wall.

She was alone. Around her feet lay the scattered remains of a torn, yellowing newspaper and a couple of old fizzy drinks cans.

It was getting hotter. She raged inside as she sat on the baked earth, but she would not cry. She dragged her snotty nose across one sleeve of her blouse. No crying! thought the girl as she scraped her cheeks where she guessed tears had streaked her dusty face. That would be a dead give-away.

In an outburst of anger she hurled one and then the other drinks can as far as she could along the length of the wall. Two magpies flew from the bushes chattering in alarm.

The girl howled.

There were people in the world who were animals – no, they were worse than animals. She remembered Manisha's eyes staring at her, fierce with hatred. Her best friend had stared accusingly at the whole world including her. And Manisha's sister in her green and gold sari had cried hysterically while the firemen in their heavy coats trudged in and out of the smoking, steaming wreck of a house that had been Manisha's home.

It had felt like a home to her too. She stayed often enough, and the Purkayastha family always made her welcome. It was better than the flat where her own mum would lecture her, while a Michael Jackson song blared from the radio.

'Dory this and Dory that,' her mother had nagged. 'You're nearly fourteen, Dorothy, so grow up, will you!'

The animals always hung around the back alleys on the estate. Sometimes they mugged a lone victim late at night in the underpass by the shops. They daubed their fascist ignorance on stairwells of the flats. Now they had poured petrol through Manisha's letterbox and set light to it. And no one would do a thing about it.

Indescribable rage filled her and she kicked at a heavy, half-rotten door in the wall. It had always resisted her attentions until now; today it splintered apart. She pushed through. There was no way she would go home tonight.

Beyond the door she was touched by the cool green light beneath the trees. It cleared her head as quickly as it seemed to shut off the nearby roar of the traffic on Western Avenue. Time had stopped here, or at least moved at a different rate.

The girl pushed through the bracken when suddenly her foot struck something hard. She looked down and for a second she thought there was an eye staring up at her.

Half hidden in the undergrowth was the head of a lion. A few feet away lay the rest of its stone body. Although the lion's features were weathered and blotched by lichen, they were still noble and regal.

The girl almost laughed in shock and revulsion: there was a large, glossy backed beetle resting on the statue's eye.

She briefly thought of childishly pencilling a pair of spectacles across the beast's stone face, but dismissed the idea as kids' book stuff.

There was something unnerving about this place. It was too cool and too dark; the overgrown garden was too lush and too quiet.

The beetle crawled off the lion's eye, over the forehead and down the petrified mane into the damp leaves on the ground.

The girl could see the crumbling edifice of an old house between the trees. The undergrowth went right up to the walls and climbed in through the black, open eyes of the windows. She walked towards the building.

Inside was an open area which must once have been an entrance hall. A shattered, stained-glass window overlooked a half-collapsed, mossy staircase; passages led into the house; doorways led to other rooms. Ivy wound in through the cracks and clambered up the inner walls. It was possible to see through a hole in the ceiling up several floors to a few spindly rafters and the sky beyond.

Picking her way over scattered planks to the other side of the area, she looked through the missing upper floors. High above her she could see a broken dome: it looked like the interior of an observatory.

The sky was turning a coppery colour: it pressed in through the rafters, threatening a storm. It was hot inside the house, but the girl felt cold inside as if something was watching. She could sense it just beyond the edge of her vision; it moved as she turned to face it.

Something fluttered.

An exotic butterfly with wings as big as fists glided past, catching the light in a flash of kingfisher blue. It had as much right to go about its business as anything else in this sub-tropical pocket of west London: she was the intruder.

The butterfly vanished into the depths of the ruin. The girl, however, could still sense something else was there.

Outside, she heard the distant roar of a DC10 taking its place in the procession of jets into Heathrow.

Inside, something slithered – something she couldn't see. Was it inside the walls? Or could it even be the walls themselves?

She watched a group of tiny crimson mites moving on a door frame, but it wasn't easy to ignore the notion that the whole place was staring at her. She had become the object of its scrutiny. It was almost creaking as it leaned inwards to get a better view of her, almost as if it recognized the unwelcome infiltrator.

The girl reached out for support and put her hand into something slimy. Her T-shirt caught on splintered wood.

She could always run, but the house fascinated as well as frightened her. It was alive. It might be as rotten and corrupt as fly-blown carrion yet it still teemed with life.

The house was angry too. Its very fabric was imbued with a sense of rage which now focused on her. Hatred was recorded in the dust and decay that she had disturbed. All around her invisible wings fluttered and unimaginable things crawled. She couldn't move.

Reality writhed about her and she defiantly struggled to find one thought with which she could defy it all. Yet all she saw were Manisha's eyes burning with hatred for the world. It didn't matter which world: her friend had to be avenged and it was she who had to make the evil and hatred go away!

The hateful, humid air closed in to stifle her, but now she understood. The wood in the house was as dry as tinder: she knew what to do.

The Doctor pondered the TARDIS's programme index. He had been sidetracked from his initial enquiry. The index was insisting that the English village of Greenford Parva was one half of a minor binary star in the Sherrin Cluster. He attempted to use the related subject heading of hamlets, but this led him only into the drama section.

Aggravated by this, he reflected that annotated text was a poor substitute for actual experience. He had not made an entry in his diary for years, which was hardly surprising because he was just too busy. The universe was at his fingertips; it was often at his throat as well. Still, that was the price he paid for minding other people's business. The universe needed a little nudge occasionally; otherwise it dawdled along and rarely fulfilled its potential.

Anyone who travelled in the TARDIS had a price to pay. However willingly any new companion walked through its doors, leaving their own world behind, and however determinedly they tried to assert control over the bizarre events in which the Doctor's travels might embroil them, one fact was inescapable: throughout time and space their lives were in the Time Lord's hands. Even the slickest of jugglers, however, could drop a skittle at one time or another.

The Doctor numbered many accomplishments in his catalogue and he rather enjoyed cultivating the image of cosmic factotum. That role, however, was only a part of it; he would hate to be pigeon-holed. Keep the public guessing was his motto, and sometimes he even surprised himself.

Call him showman, conjuror, great detective, mentor or tormentor, his speciality was to juggle the past, the present and the possible. No one was safe from that; anyone could be a potential skittle.

The Doctor rarely bothered with a safety net either; he never considered he needed one. But he didn't always ask the skittles.

Ace had learned to trust the Doctor with her life. Perhaps he was irritable with her sometimes, but that was because she didn't always come up to his expectations. She was only human after all, however hard she tried. Besides which, few people had expected much of her at all during her seventeen years.

The Doctor was the first person for a long time who had even bothered to accept her for what she was: a delinquent. She knew that and he seemed to like it that way too. There were things she understood now that she had never even dreamed of before; and yet there were still a few things she could teach the Doctor. Not everyone had their own personal professor and this was the weirdest tutorial in the history of the universe.

Ace hardly noticed the Doctor hurriedly put away a set of charts as she entered the TARDIS's control room. There he was in the same dark brown jacket, busy jumper, loud check trousers and eccentric, paisley scarf that he had been wearing for the past month. It was beyond her how his clothes managed to stay in some semblance of cleanliness, the amount of wear and tear he put them through. She occasionally wondered whether he slept in them too.

'Nearly there,' he announced, smiling impishly as he cleared the data from the index's screen. He had already given up on maps and charts; he was navigating through time and space by instinct. He paused and waited for the usual torrent of questions about destinations and dates and why. Except this time the explanations might not go down too well.

Nor, for that matter, would Ace's immodest apparel in the genteel environment to which they were heading. He would have to deal with her off-the-shoulder blouse and black trousers, but not yet. The prospect of a little light culture shock for the unsuspecting natives amused him.

Ace considered whether 'nearly there' referred to miles, light years, minutes or centuries. She guessed what he was waiting for and plumped for an easier option. 'Don't you ever take your hat off, Professor?'

The familiar grating crescendo of the TARDIS's dematerialization procedure broke in upon them, culminating in the heavy bass-drum thud which announced their arrival.

Spared from having to answer Ace's question, the Doctor leaned across the console to flick on the scanner switch. He stopped for a second and regarded Ace instead. 'I think it's time to put your powers of observation to the test.'

'OK.'

Ace was game for this. She switched on the scanner before the Doctor could stop her and turned to look at whatever image the screen would show. When the TARDIS slid them into a new location, the first glimpse was always exciting.

The scanner showed a pale, delicate, cream-coloured image of what appeared to be nothing at all. The Doctor smiled and tried to look as if this was what he had expected. He had done the right thing asking for Ace's opinion. Now it was her problem.

2

Gabriel Chase

There were always duties to perform: the smooth running of any large house required them out of necessity. Gabriel Chase was no exception to that rule, but there were also the unavoidable chores – tasks which no simple maidservant could undertake without supervision.

The lift clanked to a halt. Mrs Pritchard slammed aside the metal gate and pushed open the doors to reveal a darkened tunnel. She held her china lamp aloft and moved forward, a maid following to heel with a covered silver tray. The lamp illuminated the circular brickwork of the tunnel, revealing the daubed images of strange and long-dead creatures that were scattered along the curved walls.

They meant nothing to the housekeeper. The same light danced on the intricate black beading on the stiff black bodice above her heavy black skirt. It glittered on the mass of keys on the ring at her hip. She had only to see to the upkeep and running of the house and to cater for the whims of her master. Her eyes were dead to the world. If there was any vestige of emotion in her drained, grey face, it was a grim pride in her work and in her staff; for anything else there was simple contempt. She had her duties to perform.

They emerged from the mouth of the tunnel into a dimly lit room which was circled by dark, velvet curtains and an array of stuffed birds, each mounted on an ornate pedestal. The air hummed with a low, pulsing drone.

Mrs Pritchard halted at a desk that was scattered with

13

papers and guarded by a malevolent-looking stuffed crow. She selected one of a row of brass buttons and pressed it.

The furthest of the curtains immediately swished upwards to reveal a brick portal with a sturdy bolted door set into the granite wall. Mrs Pritchard approached the door and stared through a spyhole into the darkness inside.

'I have brought your dinner and a copy of *The Times*.'

There was a muffled rustling from inside the dungeon. Mrs Pritchard used a hooked stick to slide up a panel at the base of the door. She nodded to the maid who lowered the tray to the floor and removed the polished cover. Underneath was a china plate of chopped fruit and vegetables, a glass of red wine and an ironed edition of *The Times*.

The dungeon fell silent.

The maid was sliding the tray through the gap in the door when it was suddenly snatched from her grasp. She darted back in fright, but Mrs Pritchard controlled her own startled composure enough to slam down the panel on the cell's occupant and its scream of outrage.

Mrs Pritchard pushed to the back of her mind the questions with which she refused to plague herself. The screams from behind the door continued, accompanied by the sounds of breaking glass and china. She did not pause to consider the imprisoned creature's identity or appearance. They were unknown to her. She did not shudder to think how many times – perhaps hundreds – she had served a meal in this fashion; a meal apparently prepared for a guest, but served to a madman. There were always screams, and always she was momentarily unnerved by the brutal anguish of the cries.

Such thoughts were instantly dismissed: Mrs Pritchard had her duties to perform. The maid, thin-faced and almost as gaunt as her mistress, awaited instruction. There would be guests to prepare for – there were always guests, duties, chores, and dinners to be served. But today's tasks were complete: it was almost first light and time to sleep.

The approach to the house of Gabriel Chase only exacerbated the ill-humour of the Reverend Ernest Matthews.

The dogcart in which he had been forced to travel from Ealing railway station – there had been no suitable carriage – was exceedingly rickety and uncomfortable. It was already late afternoon and it had taken him most of the day to get this far from Oxford. The carter seemed to be deliberately driving over every bump in the lanes, but Ernest sat tight and silent, absorbing every jolt and reserving his temper for a more worthy target.

After several miles, the cart passed through the scattering of cottages and a church that made up a village. The parish of the Reverend C J Hughes recalled Ernest to himself, and this knowledge somehow gave him comfort that civilization was not so far away.

It was only a short distance further on that the cart came to a halt before a pair of iron gates set in a high brick wall. The carter refused to take his passenger any further. He muttered in surly tones that it was already getting late, all the time casting wary glances up the drive.

Ernest Matthews, his joints aching, clambered down from the cart. He found himself short of change and reluctantly had to give the driver a whole shilling. The carter took the coin with a leer and, urging the horse forward, disappeared up the lane at a pace that threatened to shake the cart to pieces.

The sun was already low in the sky, casting long shadows from the tall poplars that lined the driveway. Beyond the gates, the breeze dropped immediately and it became hot and sultry. The stifling air closed oppressively in around Ernest, but he resolutely remained encased in his heavy hat and ulster, clutching his large bag. This was not a social call; he meant business.

A proud stone lion, a symbol of the Empire, watched the road from a clump of rhododendrons to his left. The clusters of near luminous mauve flowers were unusual for September; the shrubs in the deanery garden outside Ernest's study window had finished flowering in June.

It had been a good year for wasps, too. A large, papery nest hung at the stone lion's throat. One of its inhabitants, drunk on the juice of rotting windfalls, circled the dark

15

figure of Ernest as part of its daily hunt for food. It narrowly avoided the irritated lash of his hand.

As he trudged up the drive, Ernest reviewed the circumstances which had led him to visit Gabriel Chase. During the past year there had been a series of privately published papers on the inflammatory subject of evolution. These articles had been written under the name of one Josiah Samuel Smith, a name which was unrecognized in scientific circles and untraceable in any university register.

Smith had endorsed the blasphemous theories of Charles Darwin and Alfred Wallace: theories that proclaimed mankind as the culmination of millennia of development. They disclaimed the truth of man's origins and denied he was created in the image of God. These theories had set the worlds of Victorian science and theology at each others' throats.

Ernest knew better. He was Dean of Mortarhouse College, Oxford, and his faith was unshakeable; he regularly lectured his students to that effect. Nevertheless, the gospel according to Josiah Samuel Smith was a different matter. Smith did not just oust mankind from the Garden of Eden: he presented man as a corrupter of nature itself. Man was depicted as an upstart who had clawed his way to dominion over all things, but who would be overwhelmed by the natural laws if he did not respect them. In Smith's philosophy, man was no more important than the lowliest creeping thing.

Occupied by his thoughts, Ernest did not notice the party of scuttling ants that he crushed underfoot as they hurried on their business.

Although the sun had almost gone, the still air pressed, making the garden seem like a hothouse. Ernest paused to mop his brow and massive sideburns. It was sweltering, but he could not loosen his dog-collar, a fact in which he rejoiced.

Ahead of him, the top of the house began to rise above the trees. It looked like an observatory: a stubby, circular turret with a domed spire and large arched windows set around its circumference. Ernest thought for a moment

16

that he could hear the distant grating and wheezing of some large mechanical device. He strained his eyes to see better and briefly imagined that he saw a light flashing in one of the turret windows. Then it was gone.

Ernest shook his head, refusing to despair, and set off again with all the committed zeal of a missionary standing on the heathen shore.

Ace opened the TARDIS's door and came face to face with the abstract, cream-coloured barrier she had seen on the scanner. She was counting precious moments and had lost a couple already. Then it clicked.

'Professor!' she yelled back in disgust. 'Thirty second penalty!'

The Doctor's irritated reply issued from the ship's inner dimensions. 'Just get on with it. It's all part of the initiative test.'

'You're still a lousy parker,' complained Ace. She slid out through the gap between the TARDIS and the creamy white wall that the Doctor had almost managed to land the police box against.

Ace almost forgot that she was in the middle of a test. She rounded the corner and came face to face with a pony. It was a second or two before she realized the creature was not real: it was the most beautifully crafted rocking horse she had ever seen. The creature's coat was exquisitely painted in uncannily realistic detail and its mane and tail were made of horsehair. It seemed to meet her gaze with such soulful brown eyes; it almost pleaded with her to climb up onto the polished saddle. Ace was beguiled.

'Well?' came the impatient voice from the TARDIS.

Jolted back to her senses, Ace surveyed the rest of the room. The TARDIS was standing in a tall, circular chamber with a high-domed ceiling that looked like an observatory's. Windows set into alcoves looked out from all directions. Blinds were drawn over them which covered all of the windows save for the tops. Had Ace looked through the gaps she would have seen the red clouds of a stormy sunset.

What held her attention were the toys. The place was full

of them: puppets, toy soldiers, dolls, sugar mice and a model galleon.

'Hey, playtime!' exclaimed Ace.

'Be concise!'

Ace gleefully picked up the tin model of a skating rink. The clockwork skaters immediately began to whizz merrily around in circles. She giggled. 'It's well safe, Professor.'

'Oh, very succinct. What about location?'

'It's a nursery.'

As Ace skimmed through the mass of toys on top of a long chest of drawers, she suddenly noticed they were muddled with a selection of scientific paraphernalia, all of which was old-fashioned but looked new.

'No, sorry. It could be a laboratory . . .' She looked with disgust at flasks that contained pickled human organs, a cuttlefish and a toad. 'But the kids'd have to be pretty creepy.'

Still none the wiser whether his instinct had brought him to the correct time and space, the Doctor abandoned all hope of finding out from his protégée. He adjusted his hat, picked up his umbrella and slid out from behind the TARDIS. He instantly knew he was spot on target.

'Time's up.'

Ace was just getting to grips with a monkey that shinned up a striped pole. She would have to bluff her way out of this one.

'Can't stand dead things,' she announced confidently, 'but the toys are great. It must be Victorian.'

The Doctor did not know whether to be pleased or annoyed. As usual, with all the odds stacked against her, Ace had pulled the correct answer out of the hat. He was deprived of his chance to lecture her. In revenge, he swung himself neatly into the saddle of the rocking horse and swayed back and forth, an infuriating know-all smile on his face.

'It's a surprise,' he said.

From somewhere in the depths of the house, he heard the jangling of a doorbell.

* * *

Ernest Matthews stood on the doorstep of Gabriel Chase, tugging hard on the bell pull. He regarded the weathered statue of the avenging angel that stood guard beside the steps, its sword raised in defiant warning. Ivy had begun to twine its spreading wings – a crumbling image of mortality.

He heard footsteps approaching from inside the house. The front door swung inwards.

Ernest marched through the portal, ignoring the scrutiny of the housekeeper.

'Tell your master that the Reverend Ernest Matthews has arrived,' he said.

Removing his hat and coat, he perused the hall he had entered. It was high and airy, dominated by a carved wooden staircase and a magnificent window of stained glass. The panelled walls were hung with animal trophies and tapestries which depicted hunting scenes. This was the house of a rich man – a family home passed down over generations – not the house of a quack pseudo-scientist whose writings displayed scant grasp of literary or scientific style, or even the basic rules of grammar.

Ernest's coat was suddenly removed from his grasp. He turned to stare at the housekeeper beside him. Ernest rarely had time for servants, but this one, who in normal circumstances would have been a cheerful soul, was plainly flustered by his arrival. Great heavens, he thought. How she dithered with his coat and hat, juggling them with the straw bonnet she already held.

'Well?' he snapped. 'This house is Gabriel Chase, is it not? The residence of Josiah Samuel Smith?'

The wretched woman's plump cheeks flushed even redder. 'Yes, sir. But excuse me, sir, as I understood, you would not be arriving until this evening.'

There were two other servants nearby. They were huddled in a corner, whispering anxiously: simple country girls wearing coloured shawls as if they were wrapped against the sudden chill of the descending dusk outside.

The housekeeper glanced again at the ornate grandfather clock at the side of the hall: its hands pointed at eight minutes to six.

'Madam,' insisted Ernest, 'my patience has already been sorely tried by the interminable train journey from Oxford.'

'Yes, sir. I'm sorry, sir. Only we don't get many visitors, you see.'

'Apparently not.' He fixed her with his most condescending smile. 'Now kindly inform Mr Smith, if he is at home to visitors, that I have answered his summons and am waiting.'

At last he seemed to be making the woman understand. With a deal of nervous bobbing and glancing back at the clock, she led him across the hall and through doors into the comfort of the parlour.

The two girls watched him go; knowing glances passed between them. The gas-lamps in the house had already been lit and they knew it would be dark before they reached the village. Hurry up, Mrs Grose they thought.

The deep tick of the clock marked its inexorable march towards six o'clock.

The Doctor had his feet up and his head was buried in a well-thumbed copy of Darwin's *Journal of the Beagle* – a leather-bound first edition.

While the Doctor refreshed himself on some of the details of Darwin's formative years, Ace was back on course with her assessment. She was steadily unloading the contents of a cupboard, rummaging through the brown glass bottles of chemicals: alum, borax . . .

'Let me guess,' interrupted the Doctor, breaking into her flow of thought. 'Beaver oil, salt . . . Boring, aren't they?'

'Yeah, nothing volatile or explosive.' She paused for a moment, unaware that she had been talking out loud. She sometimes had an uncomfortable feeling that the Doctor was inside her head.

'They're all preservative agents in the art of taxidermy.'

'Ugh, gross!' Ace hurriedly shoved back a more promising bottle of benzene and looked for a different line of investigation.

A polished brass telescope pointed out of one of the windows. On the table beside it lay a wooden box on a stand with a conical mouthpiece, an earpiece on a wire and a bell on the top. This was more like it, thought Ace. She poked hopefully at the archaic telephone. The absurd notion that what she needed was a Victorian phonecard passed through her mind.

'Did you know that Darwin suffered from seasickness?' mused the Doctor, his head back in the book. 'Odd that, considering his Origins.'

'How do I ring out on this thing?'

Brought back from the Beagle with a bump, he saw Ace fiddling with the telephone. She was liable to land them back in trouble at any second! He made a dive for the telephone.

'Ace! Put that down!'

She darted back, holding it out of his reach.

'It's called initiative, remember?' she retorted. 'All I want is the operator.'

The Doctor grappled hopelessly for possession of the telephone.

'You'll give us away! These days trespassers land up in Newgate!'

'The prison?'

'And it took me three weeks to tunnel out last time. Just give me the thing!'

He managed to snatch the telephone away from Ace, but his relief was cut short as a scratchy voice emerged from the earpiece.

'Who's there?'

'Sorry, wrong number,' replied the Doctor, before slamming down the receiver.

Ace bit her lip and waited for the inevitable lecture.

In the depths of the house, in a room darkened by heavy curtains, white-gloved hands replaced a receiver on its telephone stand. The owner crouched brooding over his desk, lit by the embers of a dying fire, muttering to himself: he was, after all, the best conversationalist he had so far encountered.

This event had not been anticipated in the plan of

tonight's work: surely the Reverend Ernest Matthews could not be at large in the house. Besides which, he was undoubtedly too fastidious a creature to be using such demonic apparatus as a telephone.

It was almost six o'clock; the sun was gone. Elsewhere in the house the lamps were alight. Drowsy eyelids would soon be opening again.

Nevertheless, the matter of an errant Oxford dean needed immediate attention. The dusty figure bent over the eyepiece of a brass microscope and started to adjust the flywheel.

In the hall, the two young maids gave audible sighs of relief as Mrs Grose emerged from the drawing room, having torn herself away from Ernest Matthews' incessant questions. It was three minutes to six. Mrs Grose closed the door behind her and almost ran across the hall. She ran past the watchful eyes of the grizzly bear in an alcove to place the house-keys on a side table for the night staff's overseer.

Dinner was in the oven and their day was done. There was no time now to check that all the other duties were complete. Pulling on her shawl, the housekeeper bustled the girls to the front door and out into the safety of the gathering twilight.

The door closed behind her; the key turned in the lock. Heaven help anyone still in the place after dark, she thought.

At two minutes to six Ernest Matthews consulted his gold hunter. He had already taken in the displays of mounted insects that vied with family portraits on the walls of the drawing room. Pride of place went to Queen Victoria whose picture hung above the mantelpiece, curtained like a shrine. There was a stuffed dodo in the corner of the room, its eyes beadily lifelike. From the framed photographs on the pianoforte, he picked out one face that he recognized: a young girl whose large, haunted eyes gazed from the sepia print – eyes which he knew to be the colour of sapphire.

He had discussed Josiah Smith's published papers on

evolution with several university colleagues and with other Fellows of the Royal Society. They had been prone to dismiss Smith's treatise as the ranting of an unknown eccentric. Even Darwin had coined a reputation to precede him, although as an expert on barnacles. Ernest, however, was incensed. In the hope of some contact, he had written to Smith through his publisher's address, challenging the charlatan to justify himself and even to address the Royal Society.

There had been no immediate response, but a month later, during a brief visit to London, he believed that he had glimpsed Smith.

Against his better judgment, he had been taken by a colleague to see the Royal Italian Opera at Covent Garden. The Egyptian melodramas of Signor Verdi's *Aida* were of little interest to him – a shamelessly decadent affair – but he had been intrigued by a young girl in the box opposite. She sat so still that she looked like a statue with pale skin and eyes which even at a distance were of piercing blue. Behind her, in the shadows at the rear of the box, was a dark figure which emerged only as the house lights dimmed. It hovered at the girl's shoulder during the performance but withdrew when the lights rose between the acts. Ernest had asked a flunkey about the identity of the figures. He was told that the box belonged to a Mr Josiah Smith and that the young girl accompanying him was his ward, whom he had been heard to refer to as Gwendoline.

Now the image of this sweet child was once again before Ernest in the photograph. His righteous temper freshly fuelled, Ernest sought out the servants' bell and began to ring for immediate attention.

The Doctor's lectures rarely lasted long. Ace sulkily fingered the crinoline of a china doll, while he held forth on the whys and wherefores of Victorian society. Unfortunately, this time he was warming to his subject.

'Now that you've so successfully drawn attention to our presence, there's only one thing for it.'

'Go and introduce ourselves properly?' muttered Ace.

'The Victorians are sticklers for formal etiquette. Their lives are bound by it. We'll have to leave the house immediately.'

Ace immediately worked out the Doctor's perverse logic. 'Don't tell me: so we can knock on the front door and get invited back in again.' She wondered whether it would have been easier to land the TARDIS outside in the first place.

The Doctor paused for a moment. He was certain that the brass telescope had been directed towards the window: now it pointed at him. He nonchalantly swung the instrument on its pivot so that it faced outward and watched as it swivelled back of its own accord, this time to point at Ace.

'Doctor, this isn't a haunted house, is it?' asked Ace.

The Doctor cast a sideways glance at Ace. She had not noticed the telescope; this was purely a sudden coincidental thought, although she was looking very uncomfortable about it.

'I told you I've got this thing about haunted houses.'

'Did you tell me that?' he asked innocently.

'Yes.'

'How many have you been in?'

'One was enough – never again.'

Something creaked behind her, or snorted, or neighed. The rocking horse, its eyes glinting, was slowly tipping back and forth of its own volition. Something had knocked it, thought Ace, that was all. A linnet in a cage turned its head with tiny clicking movements to look at her. Its wings fluttered and it started to twitter. It was just a toy, wasn't it?

From the depths of the house, they heard the deep bass notes of a grandfather clock begin to toll the hour.

3

Uncharted Territory

At the first stroke of six, wooden panels in the hall slid open to reveal the occupants of the stone alcoves behind them. Maids, as much a fabric of the house as the stones themselves, moved out into the soft light of the gas-lamps. They wore long skirts, starched aprons and prim caps; their thin grey faces had forgotten when they last saw the sunlight. Out they moved, swishing across the tiled hall floor and up the stairs.

The ponderous clock reached its third stroke. In the darkened study, white gloved hands touched the shoulder of a girl who sat motionless, staring into the fire.

'I think you should go and greet our guests, my dear,' whispered the voice.

The girl smiled gently, rose from her chair and glided from the room.

The sixth and final stroke from the clock lingered like the last gleam of the setting sun before it faded into the shadowy recesses of the house. Bony hands, sleeved in black lace, plucked up the keys from the hall table where Mrs Grose had left them.

Mrs Pritchard, the night housekeeper, moveed forward from the shadows to survey her staff. The night's duties were already clear in her mind. There were no scrawled messages from the day housekeeper, a simple-minded woman who was partly literate and to whom Mrs Pritchard was forced to entrust the care of her precious charge for the duration of daylight hours. The house was therefore in order.

Mrs Grose was paid enough not to question her daily instructions. The evening meal would be prepared and cooking in the kitchen. Those areas of the house which were not locked to the day staff would have been dusted and polished. It remained only to await the arrival of tonight's guest.

Mrs Pritchard's night staff silently awaited their mistress's orders, yet something was out of place: something that the housekeeper could not quite define was already at odds with her immaculate roster.

It was then she noticed the strange coat on the hatstand. At the same time the doors across the hall swung wide and the Reverend Ernest Matthews emerged from the drawing room. Immediately identifying Mrs Pritchard as a servant with some degree of authority, he began to give vent to his irritation.

'Are you aware that I have been ringing for attention since before six o'clock? I demand to see your master immediately.'

The maids, ranged up the length of the staircase, turned their heads in one concerted movement to observe the intruder. But Ernest, the battle light of the crusader in his eyes, was too preoccupied to notice the substantially different nature of this grim breed of servants. Instead, he met the stony gaze of the black-dressed, gaunt figure across the hall with a suitably withering look of his own. This housekeeper, if that was her station, was a haughty creature who clearly had ideas above her rank. He disliked intensely the way she surveyed him: a piercing glare from beneath leaden eyelids. He positively objected to the way she slowly drew nearer without any response to his demands. This insolence had gone far enough!

'Be warned, madam. Mr Smith will regret the consequences if I leave now. I am not without influence in the highest scientific circles. The condemnation of the Royal Society can be ruinous!'

Mrs Pritchard's slow approach never faltered. The maids

began to descend the stairs, gathering in behind their mistress.

Ernest stood his ground. He caught a musty scent like stale camphor that reminded him of things stored away for too long. There was still no reply.

So be it, thought Ernest, Josiah Smith's fate was sealed. Ernest would have turned to leave, but his eye was held. He would not be overruled by this ghastly apparition; she must be shown her place. All consuming outrage at the housekeeper's extraordinary audacity blinded him against her resemblance to a snake about to strike. She loomed over him, her maids clustered in her wake like impassive neophytes at a blood sacrifice. Slowly she raised her head.

'Reverend Matthews?'

A musical female voice cut into the confrontation. Mrs Pritchard stood frozen, betraying no trace of thwarted satisfaction, as Ernest turned to behold an angel emerging from one of the corridors. A young lady of no more than eighteen years was approaching, her tiny figure dressed in white and her hair pinned up, allowing only a few dark curls to frame her pale elfin face. Her eyes, even bluer than Ernest remembered, were the colour of cornflowers.

'You must forgive us for keeping you waiting, sir,' said the angel. 'I am Mr Smith's ward.'

For her age, the young lady had a very forward manner, but Ernest's venerable bones were so charmed that he was not taken back by the lack of a formal introduction.

'You are Gwendoline, are you not?' he ventured.

'Why, yes sir.' She seemed delighted. 'But please be assured, my guardian will join us shortly.'

Ernest moved closer, drawn by her presence. 'I fear that much of my discourse with him will not be pleasing to a young lady such as you.'

'But we are both anxious to meet you, sir. Won't you join me in the drawing room?' She gave so felicitous a smile that Ernest found himself willingly ushered back through the doors away from the hall. With scarcely a glance at the housekeeper, Gwendoline issued instructions for a pot of tea to be brought.

Mrs Pritchard turned and snapped her fingers. The maids followed obediently as she stalked away into the house.

Journal entry. September 19th, 1883.

. . . by some unimaginable feat of cunning, I have managed to break free of my bonds and escape from the hut where the devils who inhabit this God forsaken spot incarcerated me. I can hear their drums; the pounding never stops. It is three days now since I found myself in this forest. I am without supplies or company, but Redvers learned long ago how to survive on the provender of the bush, and he taught me everything I know. I am certain they are holding him close by and I have so much to report to him. For I have looked upon the most wondrous of things.

I must be careful how I move. Even with the drums, this is a strange, silent forest. Full of eyes, watching all the time. In places the trees grow so densely that they become impenetrable walls, but the local tribeswomen have cleared paths through them. The tree canopy is low and curtains of thick foliage in many hues hang from it. Likewise, the pathways are carpeted with thickly matted leaves and flowers. Strangest of all, the locals have carved strange totems, which litter the pathways. In the queerest of ways, they remind me of furniture. Redvers says the jungle can get to you like that, but I am no greenhorn and not prone to hallucinations. One thing spurs me forward: Redvers is trapped somewhere near, held prisoner by the evil ruler of this region. I must find him at all costs.

I can suddenly make out two figures in the clearing just ahead. With the intention of challenging them, I have wrested a native spear from where it hung on a tree beside a barometer. If they prove to be servants or confederates of the vile tyrant and assail me, it will cost them their lives . . .

Ace was still assessing her surroundings. She and the Doctor had come down two floors and still not reached ground level. The corridors in the lower part of the house were filled with every kind of stuffed bird. Their glass eyes seemed to be watching and this hardly made Ace feel comfortable, but she could not let the Doctor know it.

'We used to go to museums on school trips,' she announced. 'It was always "don't touch, don't wander off, don't get the school a bad name". Still did it though.'

They reached a junction; the Doctor licked his finger and held it up to test the air movement.

'The front door must be this way,' he said, setting off to the right.

Ace turned the corner after him and nearly walked into a large penguin-like bird that was mounted on a pedestal.

'Hallo,' she said, face to face with the bird and only inches from its razor-sharp bill. 'What's a great auk like you doing in a place like this? You got stuffed and it wasn't even Christmas.'

'Ace!' complained the Doctor, coming back to fetch her.

'See you later,' Ace told the auk as she headed along the Doctor's route. He passed her going in the opposite direction; his umbrella hooked over her arm and pulled her back.

Unnoticed by either of them, the great auk's eyes started to glow a soft pink colour.

'What do you make of that?' asked the Doctor, pointing at a small silver box he had noticed lying on the carpet. He crouched down beside it and she followed suit.

'Dunno. Looks like a jewel box.' Ace squinted as she tried to make out the initials engraved on the lid.

The Doctor produced a small instrument and pointed it at the box. The scanner gave a sonic twitter. The Doctor took a reading from a dial and put the instrument back in his pocket.

'Snuff,' he said.

Ace grimaced. 'Inhaling that stuff! I'm surprised humans made it into the twentieth century.'

'At this point they haven't . . . not yet. What else?'

'It's silver. Whose initials are RFC?' she asked making out the engraving at last.

'It's your initiative test.'

'That's why I'm asking questions.' She peered at the box again. 'When was the Royal Flying Corps formed?'

'The name wasn't used until 1912, but I'll get you a badge if you like. Ask me another.'

She reached out to pick up the box and got her hand sharply rapped away.

'Professor! I'm only looking.'

'Looking's one thing,' said the Doctor as he fished another instrument out of a pocket. Holding it like a gun, he pointed it at the box: the instrument started to emit a series of sharp crackles.

'It's radioactive!'

'Very slightly,' he mused, examining the Geiger counter's reading.

'Is it safe?'

'There's no such thing as a safe level.'

A worrying thought struck Ace. 'What about RFC?' Still crouching, she turned to face the Doctor and noticed that the sharp point of an African spear was sliding down between them.

The Doctor continued, oblivious to the threat. 'Hopefully he abandoned the box before he came to any harm.' He turned and registered the spear without the slightest flicker of surprise. 'A Zulu assegai,' he commented, 'fairly lethal.' He looked up the length of the spear to its owner.

The weary, weather-beaten face that returned his stare belonged to a man apparently in his late thirties. He had a haggard look to him. His thick, fair hair was greying and ruffled and his jacket looked slept in. Along with his bushy moustache, he had several days growth of stubble and accompanying bags under his eyes. Even so, Ace decided there was something dashing about him, despite the spear and being at least twice her age.

The Doctor guessed that the stranger was younger than he looked, but then too long in the bush could do that to a man. He had met explorers before; they always had a certain manner to them. They were fierce, enthusiastic – the correct word was intrepid. As it was, the stranger seemed more interested in poking the silver box with the tip of the spear than using the assegai as a weapon. The Doctor reckoned the newcomer was just as much a stranger in the house as they were.

'Where did you find it?' barked the stranger, betraying the public school accent that the Doctor had expected.

'Just here,' the Doctor replied, getting to his feet. 'I wouldn't touch it if I were you. This is Ace and I am the Doctor.'

The explorer was as enthusiastic as the Doctor had anticipated. 'I am a Fellow of the Royal Geographical Society,' he announced, shaking the Doctor's hand with gusto.

'Really? So am I – several times over,' responded the Doctor. They continued shaking hands and there was more than genuine delight in the stranger's eyes; there was definite relief that he had by chance encountered a fellow Fellow in this desolate terrain.

'Is it your snuffbox?' cut in Ace, who found all this old boy stuff boring.

It was only then that the explorer took in Ace's appearance. He executed a perfect triple take and then turned away in acute embarrassment.

'Please, young lady, you are barely dressed!'

'Who's undressed?' she exploded, resisting the Doctor's attempts to push her out of sight behind him.

'Excuse my friend,' he apologized, 'she comes from a less civilized clime.'

'What do you want me to do? Wrap up in a curtain?' came the annoyed voice from just behind his ear.

'Be quiet, noble savage,' muttered the Doctor. He addressed the explorer, 'I'm sure that in the depths of central Africa, you've seen far grislier sights than Ace's ankles.'

A veil of anxiety suddenly clouded the explorer's face, but before the Doctor could pursue the enquiry, Ace butted in again.

'He can't see my ankles.'

'Your boots then.' He struggled to keep her behind him,

while he spoke to the adventurer. 'You are a big game hunter, I take it?'

'I am, sir,' came the reply. 'But I've seen nothing that equals the atrocities that are rumoured about this place.'

The Doctor was taken aback by the open hatred embodied in that remark. He wondered if he dared risk divulging the house's location to Ace yet, but she was already pressing his arm.

'Is this the surprise, Professor? Because I'm not impressed.'

The explorer seemed no longer concerned by Ace's skimpy apparel. 'I must thank you, Doctor. I am grateful to have found an ally,' he interrupted.

'You are?' queried the Doctor.

'Of course. You have provided me with substantial proof at last.'

As he reached down for the snuffbox, the Doctor blocked Ace's instinctive move to stop him. There was a slight crackle of electricity as the explorer scooped up the box, as if either he or the object had discharged a measure of stored energy from one to the other. Ace was uncertain which way round it went.

Without flinching, the explorer held up the box in triumph. 'I came here to find Redvers Fenn-Cooper, the finest explorer in the Empire.

'RFC,' nodded the Doctor as the engraved initials on the box's lid glinted in the gaslight.

'I just knew he was close by. I am commanded to find him and rescue him from the clutches of that blackguard Josiah Samuel Smith.' He turned away from his audience, spear in one hand, box in the other and marched away into the uncharted regions of the house.

Ace shrugged and looked at the Doctor. Just for a second she caught him watching her, before he smiled and set off in the explorer's tracks.

Her sense of unease was reinforced. The Doctor was up to something, but then he was always up to something. He would probably call it weaving patterns on the loom of the universe; there were times when she thought she could make out what the patterns were. The Doctor was not the easiest person to be with, but Ace had learned that when his cards were closest to his chest, it was safest to stick as near to him as possible.

The glow in the eye of the watchful auk dimmed as Ace hurriedly tagged on behind the Doctor, reassured as she let him lead her into the shadows.

4

Gaslight Boogie

A crack of light widened into the gloom of the study, silhouetting Mrs Pritchard against the glow from the corridor outside.

'Light!' hissed the room's occupant, shielding its eyes with a white-gloved hand. The housekeeper closed the door and approached the desk.

'The new guest is installed in the drawing room as instructed, sir,' she intoned.

Her shadowy master leaned back in his chair from the microscope. His voice rasped out, soft but cultured, like iced silk. 'You're slipping, Mrs Pritchard, and so are your staff. There are more strangers in the house.'

It was not apparent whether this information was being absorbed. The housekeeper's blank stare betrayed nothing of her thoughts. Her master continued, 'I have had to release the other specimen, which may delay them for a while. But where is Nimrod? He should be dealing with them.'

'Nimrod has his other duties, sir.'

The truth delivered in such dull, sluggish tones only aggravated her employer further. Must he delegate everything himself? Of course he must. But a gentleman should never display his temper in front of mere servants. He, Josiah Samuel Smith, had read it somewhere. He swallowed his pride and suggested that she set two further places for dinner.

'Very good, sir,' came the reply. Mrs Pritchard turned and left the study.

Josiah leaned forward and reached for the telephone. There was no connection to be made, he simply turned a handle and heard a bell ringing at the other end of the line.

'Come along, Nimrod, you Darwin's delight,' he muttered in irritation.

Nimrod had duties that Josiah was loath to interrupt. They could be postponed, but not indefinitely. Indeed, of the entire household, only the manservant was reliable enough to perform these duties with any degree of competence. He was content to undertake the heaviest tasks, obeying his capricious master's strangest whims without question. He even swept out the locked cell, whose occupant, a hapless brute, shredded its daily copy of *The Times* to make itself a nest.

There was cruel mockery in Josiah's instruction that the prisoner should be extended this hospitality. Upstairs, Josiah, gratified in the certainty of the newspaper's fate, perused the world events reported in his own copy from the comfort of his leather armchair like any other Victorian gentleman.

Nimrod was not native to the Victorian world, but he had wit enough to understand even the darkest secrets of Gabriel Chase. He was privy to many of them, but he chose to interpret them in quasi-religious terms, a fact that Josiah used to secure obedience from his superstitious servant. The power of Nimrod's god passed all understanding, so Nimrod never argued – he just got on with it with reverence.

The telephone line clicked and a brutish voice, which spoke paradoxically with the impeccable diction of the gentlemen's gentlemen, enquired, 'You rang, sir?'

Two maids hurrying on some errand narrowly missed the Doctor and Ace, who were skulking in an alcove with two birds of paradise and a Lady Amherst's pheasant. The explorer had taken charge of their expedition and gone on ahead to scout, muttering something about the drums

35

getting louder. The Doctor thought he caught the first distant rumble of thunder in the air.

Ace watched the disappearing maids with apprehension. 'Wouldn't get me into service,' she muttered. 'Look at that uniform.'

'Housemaids aren't all curtsies and sugar plums,' observed the Doctor.

'Oh, yeah. It's got so much going for it: drudgery, exploitation, no thanks – no tips!'

'There speaks the ex-waitress,' he reminded her.

'It's all clear,' hissed a voice close behind Ace. She spun round to find that the explorer had slipped silently in beside them. His eyes were staring wider now and darting about wildly.

'This Josiah Samuel Smith of yours,' said the Doctor unconcernedly, 'I gather he's a bit of a trouble-maker.'

The explorer held up a hand. 'Can't talk here – too many eyes. Follow me.' He beckoned them along the passageway, talking indignantly at them as he went. 'Smith's ignored repeated requests to address the Royal Society on his theories.'

The Doctor tutted.

'He's been denounced as more of a heretic than Darwin,' continued the guide.

The Doctor glowed. 'Splendid! He sounds right up my street.'

Ace always reckoned that the Doctor was on a different planet, probably one just ahead of her. She was beginning to think the same about the explorer, but then she hit on the solution: he wasn't on a different planet, just a different continent.

Still clutching his spear, he had halted at a doorway and was directing them inside. 'We'll make camp here tonight,' he announced.

Ace's theories were confirmed.

The walls of the room they entered were adorned with animal trophies, the mounted heads of wild beasts which had suddenly and unexpectedly encountered a hunter's muzzle-loader. Among them, the Doctor recognized warthog, impala, eland, quagga and, almost twenty years before it had a right to be discovered, an okapi. Scattered on workbenches were further specimens of once living creatures that had found a new vocation as involuntary ornaments: a baby crocodile, the equisitely detailed and macabre skeleton of a South American tree monkey, and the curly horned head of a mountain goat with an inkwell set in the top of its skull.

The explorer surveyed the camp site. He suddenly seemed more at his ease as he leaned over to confide in his two companions. 'All the same, Smith did invite Redvers Fenn-Cooper here.'

Now he's back in the house, thought Ace to herself. But the explorer continued, 'Redvers is his sternest opponent and one of . . .'

'One of the finest explorers in the empire,' Ace butted in.

'And he hasn't been seen since,' added the Doctor, wistfully staring into the sad eyes of a chimpanzee's head.

'Perhaps he got lost on the way,' suggested Ace.

The explorer had opened a cabinet containing a rack of hunting rifles. 'Henry Stanley found Doctor Livingstone; I shall find Redvers Fenn-Cooper,' he snapped, fitting his spear into a place beside the guns.

The Doctor moved up behind him and started to run the Geiger counter up and down. It crackled alarmingly, startling the explorer, who began to wave his hand in the air in front of his face.

'Damn tsetse flies!' he complained.

Leaving him engrossed in the cabinet's contents, the Doctor checked the instrument's readings. Ace sidled up to him.

'Can we go now, Professor? This whole place gives me the creeps.'

'I thought it might,' he mused.

Ace nodded in the direction of the explorer. 'That one's a headcase. And the house is like a morgue – everything dead.'

The drums in the explorer's head suddenly exploded into

a pounding rhythm. He grasped a breech-loader by the barrel, trawled a couple of bullets from his pocket and slotted them into place. Clicking the gun shut, he turned and aimed straight at the Doctor's head.

The Doctor stared up the shaking gun barrel which was barely two feet away. Too close to palm the bullets, he thought. Really, people in as deranged a state as this should never be allowed near guns. The barrel started to waver back and forth between himself and Ace, who was pressing in at his side.

'Stop him, Doctor,' she suggested, her voice quavering.

'Tell me what else you found in the house,' he said as conversationally as he could muster, even though it effectively concentrated the line of fire on himself.

'He . . .' stuttered the explorer feverishly as he stared down the barrel. 'Redvers had some stories. The pygmies of the Oluti Forest led him blindford for three days through uncharted jungle. They took him to a swamp full of giant lizards like living dinosaurs.' He started to lower the gun, adding dismissively, 'Do you know young Conan Doyle just laughed at him. Ha! Well, that's doctors for you!'

The Doctor nodded in grim agreement, swiftly scanning his memory for anything to do with Victorian firearms.

'That wouldn't be a Chinese fowling piece, would it?' he said, reaching forward to take the weapon.

The barrel came smartly back up and the explorer began to advance, forcing the Doctor and Ace to retreat slowly around a workbench and across the room.

'We're two weeks out from Zanzibar,' he cried in despair. 'I must find Redvers!' Through the head-splitting pounding of drums he heard from somewhere the wild, urgent piping of a native flute.

'What else did you find?' urged the Doctor. Ace noticed the first hints of desperation in his voice.

'Nothing,' came the reply.

The Doctor could only persist. 'Describe it. It's all right. I'm a doctor.'

The slow advance did not relent and neither did the pounding in the explorer's head. 'Yes. There was light.'

'Bright light?'

'Burning bright! In the heart of the interior.'

'Tell me,' insisted the Doctor.

Ace slipped out of the line of fire, aware that in a moment she would be able to take this loony sideways on.

The explorer never let the Doctor out of his sights, but the haunting sounds of the drums and the flute filled his eyes with the full horror of his vision. 'It burnt through my eyes into my mind. It had blazing, radiant wings!'

Ace saw the hunter's trigger finger tighten and flung herself at him. She was caught squarely by his shoulder and tumbled across the room into a stunned heap.

The explorer hardly lost his aim; his target was now backed up against a long curtain.

Only inches from the muzzle, the Doctor began to fumble for something to distract his assailant, but all he grasped was the length of drape.

Jubilantly, the explorer began a new tale. 'Once, when Redvers was in the Congo, he faced a herd of stampeding buffalo head on. He raised his gun and with a single bullet . . .'

The Doctor suddenly launched himself sideways, dragging the curtain after him. The movement was so unexpected that the intrepid explorer was left staring directly at his own reflection, palely illuminated in the window against the darkness outside. The gun sagged and emotion drained the fierceness from his voice.

'There . . . there he is,' he whispered like a lost schoolboy. 'Redvers . . . I've found you at last, old chap. What have they done to you? You look like a ghost.'

Ace gathered herself up. She joined the Doctor beside the forlorn figure that gazed unmoving into the glass. 'Is it really him?' she asked, half afraid to intrude.

The Doctor gently removed the gun from Redvers' unresisting grasp and laid it aside. 'He's seen something his mind can't take in. A light or something. It's induced some sort of mental trauma.' He turned to Ace. 'You'd better go and get some help.'

'But that'll blow our cover,' she protested. The Doctor

thumped a bench in irritation. 'All right, all right,' muttered Ace and headed for the door.

It opened in her face and a bizarre gallery of figures brushed past her. A woman in black lace with the severest, saddest face Ace had ever seen was followed by hard-eyed maidservants. Behind them came – almost loping – a figure in the dress coat of a manservant. His shoulders were hunched and his long arms dangled at his sides. A course mass of brown hair surrounded his monkeyish face with its flattened nose and protruding jaw. The bright, brown eyes were set beneath a broad bony ridge across the forehead. Ace was so startled, she forgot to say 'Wow!'

The woman made a straight line for the explorer, who still stared at his own reflection.

The Doctor removed his hat for the first time that day, raised it and started introducing himself to the housekeeper. He was ignored. The woman was interested only in Redvers.

'Mr Fenn-Cooper, where've you been?' she enquired. 'We've been worried about you.'

'Poor old Redvers. Poor old fellow,' was the plaintive response.

The housekeeper delved into Redvers' pocket, extracted the silver snuffbox and deposited it in a pouch on her skirt by her keys.

'Come along now,' she said, gently turning him round with the affection of a nurse finding a long-lost child.

Redvers began to stumble forward, but she seized his arm, twisting it viciously up behind his back.

The Doctor's attempt to stop her was immediately blocked by a maid. 'I don't want him hurt!' he shouted, but the housekeeper was already forcing Redvers out through the door.

His voice came to them from the passage. 'Not the interior! Please, I don't want to go back to the interior!'

Ace made a dash after them. The last maid, however, gave her an icy stare and firmly shut the door on her. Ace turned back to find the manservant already in conversation with the Doctor.

'A most unfortunate mishap, sir. I trust you and the young lady are not hurt.'

'Well, we were just passing . . .' began the Doctor, but the manservant interrupted him with impeccably gracious tones.

'My master, Mr Smith, asks if you will join our other guest in the drawing room.'

So old Josiah already knows we're here, thought the Doctor. He eyed the room and spotted a dozen places to hide a camera.

'Is this a madhouse, Professor, with the patients in charge?' whispered Ace.

The Doctor studied the waiting manservant and admitted, 'Given the chance it could be bedlam.' He noticed the servant was reaching out a hairy hand to take his hat and umbrella. Passing them over, he said, 'Thank you, er . . .'

'Nimrod, sir.'

The Doctor raised an eyebrow. It was not uncommon for a Victorian traveller to return to England with an entourage of exotic ethnic origin, but looking at this servant, who bore the name of the mighty hunter and the features of a long extinct race, he wondered exactly where and how Josiah Samuel Smith went on his expeditions. He was intrigued and anxious to accept the invitation, but he only admitted to the latter with tempered enthusiasm.

He noticed that Nimrod was already looking hopefully at Ace's black jacket with all its badges; she was plainly going to cling on to it for dear life. The Doctor hardly liked to upset her too much, just yet.

'Downstairs?' he enquired cheerfully, managing to distract Nimrod's attention from the jacket and to look, despite recent events, as if a Victorian tea party might be fun.

Gwendoline wondered how much longer it would be before her guardian made an appearance. Taking tea with the Reverend Ernest Matthews was becoming something of an ordeal. They had discussed the weather, which he found oppressive; his journey from Oxford, which had been most disagreeable. Gwendoline wondered about showing him the collection of insects. She was sure he would like them, but Uncle Josiah had insisted that the dean should be confined to the drawing room.

After the pleasantries, his third cup of tea and slice of seedcake, Ernest, who was being extremely attentive, began to question her. He sounded like an overbearing governess.

He told her that Josiah Smith had achieved a certain reputation for the outspoken nature of his work. She protested that Uncle Josiah was a wonderful naturalist: he brought the whole world of living things into the house. Gwendoline began to strok the head of the stuffed dodo with affection – some of them were like her best friends.

Ernest could restrain his curiosity no longer. 'But you leave Gabriel Chase sometimes?' he ventured. 'Did I not see you last month at the Italian opera in London?'

Gwendoline seemed confused. She began to stutter. 'Was I? I don't . . . cannot . . .' Her fingers began to twist the chain of a locket that hung about her neck.

'At Covent Garden,' he reminded her with disdain. 'The opera was *Aida*. Signor Verdi wrote the music, if that's what they call music these days.'

'Oh yes, sir.' Gwendoline's thoughts suddenly cleared and she began to apologize. 'Sometimes I forget the simplest things. It was so dramatic and beautiful.'

'But while you watched the opera, your guardian remained in the shadows at the back of your box. He seemed more intent on watching the audience through his opera glasses.'

Gwendoline gave a forced smile. 'Those are his field trips, sir. He likes to study specimens at first hand, but too much light is painful to him.'

Ernest was no longer concerned with the details of this mystery. They were merely symptomatic of a greater, insidious evil that gnawed at the foundations of society. Because Gwendoline was threatened, he could conceal this from her no longer. He assumed the sternest of tones.

'My dear child, this is no place for an innocent. Your guardian's profane theories have made him many enemies.

In truth, he is a heathen charlatan and must be exposed as such!'

'But Uncle Josiah is a good man!' cried the object of his attention, fingering her locket in desperation. 'And he is a great naturalist too!'

'So you keep saying.'

'You will see when you meet him!'

The doors from the hall opened and a manservant of the lowest origins entered. He was followed by an impish figure who was dressed in a dark jacket with flamboyant accessories that marked him out as the dangerous eccentric whom Ernest had come so far to meet.

'At last,' muttered the dean, deserting Gwendoline and advancing to confront his adversary without delay. 'So you finally consent to meet me, sir,' he announced sarcastically. 'I am grateful for your hospitality.'

The Doctor smiled and half offered a genial hand. Seeing that it was not going to be shaken, he nonetheless said, 'How do you do. Thank you for coming,' because it seemed to be the sort of thing that kept Victorian humans happy.

There came the first defined peal of approaching thunder.

Ernest had been determined to waste no time condemning his enemy, but his jaw dropped as he noticed the Doctor's companion: a creature who, without the slightest decorum, was dressed in what appeared to be briefest of undergarments.

'Good Lord!' he exclaimed – the best he could manage at the time.

The Doctor knew that any Victorians' reaction to Ace would be amusing. As he formally introduced her, he surmised that he could not have found a more likely candidate than this pillar of the clerical establishment. Ernest's reaction was as extreme as the Doctor had hoped, and he soon found words to express it.

'I see that all the rumours about you are true,' he protested. 'You have no shred of decency – even parading your shameless wantons in front of your guests.'

'Does he mean me, Professor?' asked Ace.

'Professor!' exclaimed the dean. 'And at which scholarly seat did you obtain this latest status?'

'The Ace School of Etiquette?' suggested the Doctor with a sly grin. The girl giggled. 'There are so many to choose from,' he added.

Ernest was getting into his stride now. 'I have it!' he mocked, pointing at Ace. 'This is some experiment related to your mumbo-jumbo theories. Perhaps she'll evolve into a young lady.'

Everybody down, thought the Doctor, sensing Ace's hackles rising.

'Who are you calling a young lady, bogbrain?' she exploded, astonishing Ernest so much that he had to sit down. There was a simultaneous giggle from across the room where Gwendoline had taken refuge behind the piano.

'Not much luck so far,' concluded the Doctor, adding quickly. 'Quiet, Eliza, and be a good girl. I'm making small talk.'

Nimrod had hovered at the door ready to intervene, but the Doctor abruptly dismissed him.

'Thank you, Nimrod. There's still some tea in the pot. See if you can find a couple more cups, thank you very much.'

The manservant was surprised to find himself walking out of the door, clutching something the Doctor had slipped into his hand. He looked at the item, was startled, and came face to face with Mrs Pritchard who stood glowering in the hall.

'The master is waiting for you,' she intoned, as more thunder rumbled ominously.

Nimrod instinctively looked up to where the sky had always been before the advent of ceilings. There was no smell of rain. This was no ordinary storm brewing; his interrupted duties must not be delayed too long. He clutched the token that the Doctor had given him, unable to grasp how the stranger could deduce so much of his past. He wondered what law decided the form that a sign from the gods might take.

'More cups for the guests,' he said and left Mrs Pritchard to serve the tea.

Gwendoline was starting to enjoy the upheaval caused by the new arrivals. Skirting the still dumbstruck Ernest, she approached the Doctor with a teasing smile. 'Sir, I think Mr Matthews is confused.'

'Don't worry,' confided the Doctor, 'I'll have him completely bewildered by the time I've finished.'

'I'll help,' chipped in Ace.

It was time to tell a few white lies to their hostess, if only to explain their unexpected arrival. The Doctor confessed that they had suffered a little trouble with their carriage and that Ace could not possibly stay to dinner looking like that!

'Who says,' complained Ace, surprised at the assumption that they might get an evening meal too.

'Perhaps you could find her some more appropriate apparel,' suggested the Doctor.

'Gladly, sir,' was the reply. Gwendoline began to lead Ace towards the door. 'Come, Alice, you may borrow something of mine.'

'It's Ace, actually,' said Ace, looking back for a reassuring nod from the Doctor. 'But thanks anyway.'

'And Alice?' he called after them.

'I'm not wearing a bustle!' came the retort.

'At least try for a bit of parlour-cred!'

5
Josiah's Web

Nimrod had hastened to the dimly lit study with the intention of begging leave to return to his duties. Instead, he found his master crouched over his all-seeing microscope in a state of agitation.

'What did he give you, Nimrod?' was his sole greeting, as lightning flickered beyond the drawn curtains.

'Sir?'

'What did the strange little professor give you? I saw him.'

Nimrod made no attempt at pretence. There were few secrets from his master. He was still clutching the Doctor's gift and held it out in his open hand.

'The tooth of a cave bear,' muttered Josiah. 'And so?'

'It has magical properties,' insisted Nimrod with the utmost reverence. Josiah leaned forward to take the tooth, but the manservant withdrew his hand and closed it tightly.

'I'm sorry, sir,' he said.

Josiah paused for a second, his eyes meeting Nimrod's in a momentary flash of anger. Lightning hissed outside the window.

'Primitive fiddle-faddle,' he scoffed, but Nimrod was adamant.

'It is a totem of great power bestowed only by the greatest elders of my tribe.'

Josiah sneered again. A furious roar of thunder tore out

of the night as if in answer. The glass prisms beneath the unlit gas-lamps rattled and sparkled in the firelight.

Without breaking from Josiah's glare, Nimrod slowly placed the tooth in his waistcoat pocket.

'The Burning One is restless tonight,' he said.

Josiah snapped angrily at his servant's defiance. 'I have need of you here, Nimrod. Stay within call.'

'Very good, sir.' Nimrod bowed his head in acceptance, but he suspected that Josiah had made a serious error of judgment.

As the manservant left the study, Josiah's white-gloved hands unfolded a pair of spectacles with lenses of black, smoked glass.

Nimrod extracted the scored, yellow tooth from his pocket and held it tightly in his fist. Beyond hope, he clutched a link with his long-lost home. Josiah knew nothing of the token's portent. True, he had taught Nimrod much in terms of survival in this changed, tamed world. Nimrod had learned the lore of language and etiquette and subservience, and for these he was grateful. But there were older memories that he could not forget, lore that few people of this age remembered. No one here listened to the wildness of the woods and the waters. Their thoughts were turned in on themselves so that they never heard the endless, ruthless struggle of life itself in the air and the earth. Only Nimrod heard.

Tonight the Burning One, Nimrod's god, stirred angrily in his dreams and a stranger carried a token of ancient magic to the house of Gabriel Chase. But how could he tell if the Doctor was a harbinger of good or ill omens? Nimrod was not born a seer; he was not able to interpret the signs like the wise men of his tribe. He heard only the wind's song in the branches and saw the patterns in the embers of the dead fire; he did not understand their meaning. He stared at the tooth, willing it to speak its secrets in his head. It had come to him and he must understand.

Uncertain whether to stay close to his master and therefore near to the Doctor, or to attempt to placate the growing anger of his god, whatever sacrifice that might mean, Nimrod resolved to wait. In this place, time flowed faster than in the old wild world, even though the sun still travelled the same course. The days chased each other more swiftly. Nimrod would be the stationary point which events moved around. He would watch as he always had watched and listened, because he would then have new tales to tell.

Wearily, he sat down on the stairs and waited for something to happen. The thunder rolled, the clock ticked steadily forward and from the drawing room came the sound of voices raised in anger. Nimrod listened, plucking idly at a baluster where it was starting to come into leaf.

'Let me guess,' revelled the Doctor, encouraging Ernest's misplaced tirade. 'My theories appal you, my heresies outrage you, I never answer letters and you don't like my jumper.' He helped himself to a piece of seedcake from the tea tray.

'You are a worse scoundrel than Darwin, sir!' retaliated Ernest.

'Just call me Doctor,' said the Doctor and finished the cake. He seated himself on the piano stool and flexed his fingers. 'Do excuse me. It's a long time since I tickled the ivories.'

So saying, he launched into a heavy boogie-woogie: he pounded at the keys; not too much pedal or he would lose the stomp. He was just getting into the feel of the thing when he glanced up to catch the open-jawed and aghast reception he was getting from his audience. Ernest Matthews, his senses under unimaginable assault, was, for the second time that day, rendered speechless.

The Doctor smirked. 'So sorry. I was forgetting the time.'

Without a quaver's pause, he dropped effortlessly into some Beethoven. The gentle opening bars of Ludwig's Moonlight Sonata seemed to relax the distraught dean. The pianist smiled knowingly as the sinuous line in the upper hand began to weave a mysterious aura through the room. As the silvery melody rose and fell, the gas-lamps seemed to dim in sympathy around them. Glancing beyond the enrapt Ernest's shoulder, the Doctor saw a door swinging slowly open in the clustering shadows at the far end of the room. He continued playing as dark undertones began to assert themselves in the lower register of the music. A figure was emerging from the gloom of the house. Its hair was white and long; its skin pale and leech-like. It wore a night-blue, velvet dinner-jacket and black, pebble-lensed spectacles that looked like tiny craters on its wizened, wicked face. As it groped its way into the half-light, grasping at the back of a chair for support, the Doctor saw that the creature's clothes were covered in strands of cobwebs.

The music stopped and Ernest turned, his trance broken as the Doctor rose to greet the figure. 'Josiah Samuel Smith, I presume,' he said, crossing the room. 'I am the Doctor, and this is . . .'

Josiah's own cracked voice took up the formalities, '. . . the Reverend Ernest Matthews of Mortarhouse College, Oxford. Your servant, sirs. Welcome to Gabriel Chase.' He bowed to them, spreading his arms in greeting, at once reminding the Doctor of a spider welcoming flies into its parlour.

'You can't beat a dramatic entrance,' declared the Doctor.

'But it was remiss of Gwendoline not to have introduced you to each other properly,' apologized Josiah.

Ernest Matthews scowled and sat down again. He wanted no part in these childish charades. His dignity had already been compromised, but the battle light of his crusade was not yet eclipsed. He watched Josiah Smith turn away to close the door and saw the Doctor run his finger down the back of their host's cobwebbed jacket. 'Dust to dust,' he heard him mutter.

Turning back, Josiah regarded his guests. 'Two scholars,' he said with satisfaction. 'I never fail to marvel at the abundance of sub-species in the genus *Homo Victorianus*.'

Ernest rallied himself to confront Josiah, but he found the Doctor with his enfuriating smile, already tapping at one of the glass cases of mounted insects on the wall.

'Fascinating moths,' he enthused.

Josiah seemed eager to discuss such things at the expense of his other guest. 'I recently made a study of this species,' he said. 'You will notice that there is a wide variation in markings from countryside to town.'

The Doctor managed to look surprised. 'Extraordinary. And have you reached a conclusion?'

'I am certain that they are adapting to survive the smoke with which industry is tainting the land.'

Ernest had endured enough. He rose to his feet and vied with the storm outside for attention.

'I wrote to you, sir, requesting an explanation for the extremity of your theories. You requested my presence, so I have come . . . only to be subjected to a series of insults from your guests and your household!'

He suddenly found his arm taken and the Doctor muttering advice in his ear. 'Never bite the hand that feeds you, dean, at least not until after dinner.'

Ernest pulled free of the Doctor's grip and turned back to face Josiah. 'Well, sir? I demand an answer!'

Josiah grinned. 'I perceive, Ernest, that you are an academic and a city man. You certainly shout like one.' His white gloves gripped the back of the chair like claws as he hissed, 'In the country, you will find it prudent to converse in more restrained tones!'

'I won't listen to such nonsense!' insisted the dean.

The Doctor shrugged. Because he appeared to have assumed the role of umpire in this feud, he felt obliged to play both sides off against each other for maximum effect. 'It's just his stubborn genetic code,' he advised Josiah. 'The inability to adapt to new ideas is the fate of too many doomed species.'

'No one asked your opinion, sir!' objected Ernest.

'Nevertheless, I suggest you concede to my wisdom . . . and button it!'

Ernest looked astonished, but the Doctor just smiled nonchalantly and added, 'Why not read Darwin, instead of just condemning him.'

A squall of wind rattled the windows. Through the noise

50

the Doctor thought he could hear the distant scream of a terrified explorer.

Ace was not sure she could cope with Gwendoline: she had met rich kids with proper educations before and they had always been real pains. Gwendoline was a bit of a prim and proper job too. She was friendly enough as she led Ace up through the house to her room, but she never asked where Ace had come from. When Ace asked exactly where the house was, she looked confused and came out with some spiel about how the place belonged to her guardian, and how good he was, and a great naturalist too – Ace would see when she met him.

Ace did not exactly like Gwendoline's bedroom either. It was filled, as she expected, with chintzy antiques, a dressing-table, a delicate porcelain washing bowl and a jug. There was a stack of hatboxes on the wardrobe. Prominent among all the objects, however, was a beautifully intricate and detailed doll's house. Looking closer she saw that it was peopled by a family of stuffed red squirrels in Victorian dress.

Gwendoline seated herself at the dressing table and suggested that Ace might try on anything in the wardrobe that took her fancy.

At first glance, Ace could see only a load of Victorian fancy dress. All of it had full skirts and tight bodices, none of which could be worn without a corset. She decided that getting through to Gwendoline would be hard going.

She was about to give up on the clothes too, when Gwendoline suddenly gave her the weirdest look and began to giggle.

'O, Alice, we shall be friends, shan't we?' she said, opening an enamelled box on the dressing table and holding it out. The box was full of cigars.

'Go on, take one,' she insisted, going through the brands. 'Regalia, Aurora, Eureka . . . Uncle Josiah chose them especially for me.'

Well weird, thought Ace. She muttered some excuse

about trying to give them up, but the ice was broken and she burst into giggles too.

'You can call me Ace,' she said. 'And I thought Victorians would be stuffy!'

'That's just uncle's collection,' said Gwendoline. They fell about laughing.

As they started going through the dresses again, Ace plucked up courage to ask about Gwendoline's guardian. The girl looked confused again and began to finger her locket.

'Father . . . he went to Java,' she said.

'Java?'

'Yes. He went away so suddenly . . . and my dear Mamma. I don't really remember her.' The plaintive look that she gave suggested that perhaps Ace might know better than she did. Gwendoline added quietly, 'Sometimes I wish I'd gone to Java too.'

The last remark was said with such resigned despair that Ace was momentarily lost for words. Parents were a subject that she always kept well to the back of her mind.

'Look. These clothes . . .' she said hurriedly. 'I mean, no offence, but they've no style, have they? You wouldn't catch me dead in them.'

Gwendoline buried her face in her hands and began to sob helplessly.

Me and my mouth, thought Ace. 'I'm sorry, Gwendoline. I didn't mean it. I just didn't think,' she said, putting an arm round the girl's shoulders.

'It's not you,' Gwendoline choked.

'Well, who then?'

'The Reverend Ernest Matthews told me that if I stay here in this house, my soul will be consigned to eternal damnation.'

'Self-righteous toerag!' exploded Ace. She pulled a grubby tissue out of her sleeve and passed it to Gwendoline.

'He is . . . very disagreeable!' concurred Gwendoline between sobs.

Ace hugged her for a second and thought about the best way to get revenge on Ernest.

'Take no notice of him,' she said. 'He's just a stuffed up bigot; he can't hurt you. He had a go at me too.'

She looked at the wardrobe. It was no good. She would have to find something to wear or the Doctor would throw a wobbler. She began to root through the clothes again, seeing nothing she remotely liked, until she found just what she hadn't been looking for right at the back. She knew it was right.

Outside the thunder, which had relented for a while, unleashed itself with fresh fury.

It took a couple of minutes to convince Gwendoline that she could wear what Ace had found and not much longer to change their clothes. Despite fits of giggles, Gwendoline was surprisingly proficient at pinning a few neat tucks in the material and the effect was better than Ace had expected. She had just struggled with an unco-operative bow tie and beaten it into submission when a frightened voice behind her whispered her name.

She turned to see Gwendoline staring at the long curtain covering the window. Something was moving about half-way up behind the drape. Gwendoline paused for a second, reckoning she knew the cause.

'Redvers? Is that you?' she said.

The curtain continued to move, not slowly, but with a fast, fluttering pulse. Gwendoline was transfixed.

Ace darted forward and threw back the drape. She revealed a small bird which was desperately beating its wings against the glass.

Lightning blazed in through the window, accompanied by a stone-splitting crack of thunder. The bird dropped to the floor and lay fluttering on its back at Ace's feet. The beats of its wings grew slower and finally stopped altogether.

Ace reached down to touch it, but drew her hand away with a look of distaste.

'It's just a toy. Look, one of the toys,' she said, but the toy, like those in the observatory at the top of the house, was a little too real.

Gwendoline knelt down by the bird with a look of grief

53

on her face. 'Poor thing,' she said. 'It was one of my friends. And it's such a long way to go to Java.'

The storm crashed again and from somewhere close by, they heard the terrified cry of a man beyond the end of his wits.

'Come on, something's happening!' Ace said, heading for the door.

Gwendoline faltered: until now it had been only a game. 'Wait! I can't wear this,' she called.

'Course you can,' came the reply as Ace disappeared up the passage. Gwendoline heard the scream again and followed.

Against the screams and the rolling thunder, Ace could hear a gushing, rasping noise that grated in her head. She rounded a corner and saw the housekeeper in repose, a candle in one hand, her head reclined against a closed door and her grip firmly on the handle. White light seeped under the door and the gushing sound came from inside.

Immediately, Gwendoline was at Ace's shoulder. 'Mrs Pritchard? What's going on?' she demanded.

Without moving her head to look at them, Mrs Pritchard's dead voice replied, 'The door is jammed, miss.'

There was another scream from inside the room, to which the housekeeper paid no apparent attention.

'Let me do it,' said Ace, grabbing at the handle.

Mrs Pritchard's arm thrust out to restrain Ace and her head turned sluggishly to fix Ace with a baleful stare. The eyes narrowed as she took in the girls' dinner suits and bow ties.

Ace returned the glare and stepped back to get a decent swing at the door with her foot. There was another cry and the light under the door burned more fiercely.

'Ace!' The Doctor dashed along the passage and pulled her clear. 'That's no way for a Victorian lady . . .' he took in her clothes and corrected himself, '. . . gentleman to behave!'

'I'm no gentleman!' she protested.

'That's still no excuse to wreck the joint.'

Ace, however, was not listening. She was staring at

Josiah, who had come up the passage followed by Nimrod. His white face with its parchment-like skin leered at her from behind the black glass spectacles before he turned towards the others.

'Gwendoline, is this a metamorphosis?' he croaked, fingering the sleeve on her black dinner-jacket.

'It was Ace's idea,' she replied, proudly grinning at her new friend.

Josiah turned back to scrutinize Ace again. She paled at his look and clung on to the Doctor for protection.

The thunder boomed, but there were no more cries from the room, only the nerve-jangling flood of sound. So intense was the glare from behind the door that the grain of the wood stood out darkly on the opaque, glowing panels.

Josiah motioned Nimrod towards the door. The energy surged in power as Mrs Pritchard moved aside to allow Nimrod access and her candle exploded like a firework, flinging sparks into Josiah's face. He fell back with a cry.

The Doctor and Ace exchanged worried glances.

'I like the tuxedo,' said the Doctor.

Nimrod set his shoulder to the door and began to heave all his weight against the barrier. It was then that Ace noticed a loud clicking coming from the Doctor's jacket.

'You're crackling, Porfessor,' she whispered in his ear. He plunged his hand into his pocket and produced the Geiger counter. Its display uncontrollably flashed through an impossible range of figures.

'Get behind me,' ordered the Doctor, pushing Ace back and covering her eyes with his hand.

Nimrod began to heave the door open. Cold light sliced into the passage, draining the colour from everything it caught in its glare. As the group recoiled, the Doctor darted through the door before he could be stopped.

There was a man crouched on the bare boards of the empty room. He was unable to move; his arms were bound in a strait-jacket. The Doctor knew the figure must be Redvers Fenn-Cooper, but the blinding light thickened the air with an icy haze which obscured everything but the boldest shapes.

An aurora of a hundred shifting shades of white emanated from a core of such brilliance as the Doctor had never seen. It was like looking into knives or the furnace of a frozen sun. The core burned on the floor beside the shaking form of Redvers, who crouched with his back against the heart of infinite, primal light.

As if disturbed by the Doctor's intrusion, the sound began to die and the air to thin of the light mist. Nimrod shielded his eyes and struggled through the doorway.

'I'm sorry, Doctor,' he gasped, trying to pull the intruder away. But the Doctor wrenched his arm free and crouched by the explorer.

'Redvers! What did you see? You must tell me!' he demanded.

As Nimrod took the Doctor's arm, Redvers raised his trembling head and slowly opened his eyes.

'Poor old Redvers,' he confided, staring into the Dcotor's face. 'He was so frightened his hair turned completely white. You know, they had to lock him away.'

Whether bleached by the light or shock, Redvers' yellow hair was now pure white. He looked down at the floor. The core of light had dwindled to a glimmer inside the open silver snuffbox from which it had emerged – Redvers' snuffbox, which he had watched the chief tribeswoman in black lace set down so carefully beside him, smiling as she did so.

Ace tried to push her way into the room, but Mrs Pritchard seized hold of her plait and twisted it viciously. 'This way, please,' she muttered through gritted teeth and dragged Ace yelling down the passage.

'You must leave, Doctor,' insisted Nimrod.

This time the Doctor allowed himself to be ushered to the door. He thought to offer Redvers further help, but found the door closing in his face.

Alone in the room, Nimrod crouched beside Redvers and took the explorer's shoulders in his great hairy hands. 'Mr Fenn-Cooper,' he asked with the greatest urgency, 'tell me what you saw. I must know.'

* * *

The Doctor pursued Mrs Pritchard as she escorted Ace through the house. He was more concerned about Redvers' welfare than that of his companion and he demanded that the explorer should be moved to a place where he could be nursed in safety.

'Out of the question,' was the only reply the housekeeper would repeat.

Josiah was waiting in the drawing room with Gwendoline and Ernest when Mrs Pritchard finally thrust Ace from her grip. The storm had at last vented its rage and was rumbling into the distance. To Ace's surprise, the Doctor suddenly dropped his angry questions and went into what she supposed to be parlour mode.

'Be assured, Doctor, Redvers will be well taken care of,' Josiah informed him.

'I bet he will,' snapped Ace. The Doctor laid a settling hand on her arm but she still wanted to give them a piece of her mind.

Nimrod entered from the hall and approached the Doctor direct.

'Doctor, I can personally vouch for Mr Fenn-Cooper's safety. He is being made comfortable and will come to no harm.' He revealed the tooth of the cave bear in his palm as a token of good faith.

The Doctor nodded and looked Nimrod directly in the eye. 'Only the madman may see the clear path through the tangled forest,' he said.

Bowing reverently, Nimrod intoned the correct response. 'So has it always been.'

'Nimrod,' interrupted Josiah sternly, 'you still have other duties to perform.'

Watching the manservant leave, the Doctor restrained himself from following. He reckoned that they hadn't seen even half of the house's secrets yet, but it would be better to allow them to emerge a little at a time. Besides which, he wanted to see how quickly Ace could assess the situation and whether she could cope with it. It had taken him a good deal of guess-work using temporal, thirty-seven dimensional charts and his and the TARDIS's joint nose for trouble to arrive at Gabriel Chase. Ace, did she but know it, potentially knew more than he did about the house, although he was already grasping the essential facts. He did not like their implications.

He was aware of Ace's chin resting on his shoulder as she also followed Nimrod's departure. 'He's a Neanderthal, isn't he?' she whispered.

He nodded. 'The finest example I've seen this side of the Pleistocene era.'

'I am no longer surprised by anything in this place,' announced Ernest, who was becoming vexed at the lack of attention he was receiving. He was ignored as Josiah muttered private instructions to Mrs Pritchard.

The Doctor waited for Ace to ask him why Nimrod was there. He was surprised when the question did not come and wondered whether she was working out the answer for herself. He hoped she would tell him too. To his annoyance, he noticed that in their absence, Ernest had finished off the rest of the seedcake.

Suddenly, the Doctor remembered Ace's dinner-jacket and remarked, 'Did I ever take you to see Georges Sand?'

'Who's he?' she asked.

'She was Frédéric Chopin's girlfriend. How about *Der Rosenkavalier*? *Die Fledermaus*?'

'Opera!' she grimaced.

He shrugged and tried again. 'Vesta Tilley?'

Ace thought for a moment and then concluded triumphantly, 'Burlington Bertie from Bow!'

'Hmm. And yours needs some attention,' he commented, affectionately straightening her tie. The male impersonators of the Victorian music hall were probably not what Ace had in mind, but she had nevertheless skilfully adapted her appearance to suit her surroundings on her own terms, which was just as well, thought the Doctor.

From somewhere nearby he heard the clink of metal. A couple of centuries before, the sound could have meant that instruments of torture were being set up. These days it would be the laying of cutlery for dinner.

Josiah finished his discourse with Mrs Pritchard and turned back to the company.

'Shall we go in to dinner, my friends?' he smiled.

'This way please,' said Mrs Pritchard. She led the way through another door into the blood-red dining room.

Ernest rose and went willingly, followed by Gwendoline and Ace. The Doctor mused for a moment on the perversities that made such a satisfying theatrical experience of tragedy. And now it was dinner time in Josiah's house; how very civilized the business of torture had become. Breaking from his reverie, he saw his host waiting upon him. Josiah leered, his arm outstretched like a showman indicating the way.

Ah well, head on the block again, thought the Doctor. He brushed some crumbs of cake from his jumper and went into dinner.

6
That's the Way to the Zoo

Even as he loped along the painted tunnel towards the chamber, Nimrod knew that he had been wrong to delay. Redvers Fenn-Cooper had said little that Nimrod did not already know: 'The burning light is angry. It sleeps in the heart of the interior.' But the explorer had good cause to remember: it was just a week since he had arrived at the house as another of Mr Smith's guests and managed to break into one of the restricted areas.

Nimrod had got the blame for that, but he suspected that Fenn-Cooper had slipped past the obstacles far too easily. From Mrs Pritchard's triumphant smirk, he supposed that she had been indulging her malicious streak again. There was no love lost between Nimrod and the housekeeper. If she could cause him trouble, she would. If, in this case, it also caused Redvers Fenn-Cooper to see just enough to drive him insane, then that only deepened her satisfaction.

'And if it wakens, we shall all burn,' Redvers had raved, speaking aloud the fears Nimrod had tried to ignore. The manservant left him babbling about doctors, living stones and Doctor Livingstone. Pausing only to stop in the drawing room to reassure the Doctor of Redvers' safety, Nimrod had made his way with dread to the resting place of the Burning One.

The curtained chamber showed no immediate signs of damage: the grotesque stuffed birds still perched on their pedestals and the furniture was all correctly positioned.

There was a slight haze, however, and the air was charged with tension. The Neanderthal could hear the same niggling sound that accompanied the manifestation in the empty bedroom. Beneath it there was a deep grinding noise as if the granite walls of the chamber were shifting in agitation.

He reached the mahogany desk at the chamber's centre and, pushing aside a pile of paperwork, pressed the series of brass buttons on the desk top. The curtains surrounding the area swished up in sequence to reveal the walls behind.

The chamber was octagonal, apparently hewn out of living rock. The angle between each wall was bisected by a heavy stone buttress, its surface glistening with crystalline fragments. Outcrops of chrysoprase and rose quartz crystals clustered at points around the chamber. The walls were inlaid with wide screens that flickered with lozenges of coloured light – a living stained glass whose colours constantly changed and merged. The light caught in the prisms of the elegant chandelier hanging from the ceiling and was refracted through the shimmering haze like neon shoals of tiny darting fish.

In front of one wall was a carved slab of stone like a sloping altar. Nimrod fingered the coloured crystal rods that grew from it; they hummed and flickered, rising and falling in no particular sequence.

Reverently laying his hands on the slab, Nimrod bowed his head to an illuminated oval cell as wide as a man is tall which was set in the wall beyond it. The cell's mouth was sealed over by a crusty opaque membrane behind which a shadow moved and turned against the glow, restlessly shifting its shape and form. Nimrod felt the waves of energy flowing out through the chamber. He tried to meet its thoughts, to appease its anger, but he could not commune with it. His instinct as a hunter drew his concentration elsewhere; he knew that he was being watched.

He left the slab and crossed the chamber to the dungeon door. There was no sound from the darkness inside, but he still tested that the bolts were firmly in place. The creature incarcerated inside was probably too terrified to make its usual grunts and snarls, even if lately the howls had become more like plaintiff wailing.

'Poor silent brute,' muttered Nimrod.

A deep rumbling note drew him back to his place at the altar slab. Behind him an eye appeared at the spyhole in the door, staring out from its tiny dark prison world into the world of light.

'Not . . . silent . . . now!' spat a voice, sounding each word as if articulating it for the first time.

Nimrod was too absorbed in his devotions to hear. He knelt at the slab, willing his mind into thoughts of propitiation and atonement, trying to appease the disturbed shadow behind the membrane. At last the restless movement and fierce glare settled into a gently pulsing glow.

The eye at the spyhole watched the manservant and then squinted as far round as it could see to an alcove curtained off from the rest of the chamber. The creature had only to whisper instructions. It had links to the outer world and was only now learning to use them.

'Move yourselves. Move!' it hissed.

It saw the curtain stir and draw back as something lumbered out of the alcove. The creature at the spyhole half saw the thing and half saw through the thing's eyes. The thing was an extension of the prisoner's own self; it stumbled towards the kneeling manservant.

'Move! Move!'

It took all of the captive's will to control the thing's flailing limbs as it moved closer and closer to Nimrod. It wore a dusty gentleman's suit and black shoes, and carried a cane which it raised in its white gloved hand above its grey, bloated, reptilian head. One stroke and the Neanderthal was knocked senseless.

'Did that hurt?' came the voice. The prisoner stared through the thing's eyes at the body of its jailer. 'Good!'

Through its will it turned the stumbling figure of the thing towards the dungeon door.

'Here!' it ordered. 'Here! Move! Now open door!'

The thing slowly began to draw back the heavy bolts and heave the door open. The prisoner squealed in pain as the glare flooded into its tiny dark world from the new world outside. Slowly and painfully, it groped its way into the light and rose unaided on to its two rear legs. It stared at the grotesque swaying thing that had released it and then looked again through the thing's eyes. It saw itself for the first time and began to scream.

There did not seem to be any soup for dinner or even any entrée, although each place at the table was laid with enough cutlery for six courses. Ace hated formal dinner parties like this, because she never knew which knife or fork to use first.

Josiah and Ernest faced each other as opponents across the length of the table, flanked on one side by Ace and the Doctor and on the other by Gwendoline.

And in the red corner . . . thought the Doctor as the maids busied themselves at the sideboard.

At a nod from Josiah, Mrs Pritchard set a dish into the centre of the table. The host lifted a large spoon, apparently prepared to do his guests the honour of serving them himself.

'I hope you have a taste for calves' brains, young lady,' he said with a smile to Ace.

She gulped and glanced at the Doctor, who was scrutinizing the dish with what looked more like scientific curiosity than a gourmet's enthusiasm.

'I'm still trying to work out where this place is,' said Ace, hoping to stay within the bounds of Victorian etiquette and change the subject at the same time.

'And I am still awaiting an explanation for your unholy and blasphemous theories,' said a voice from the far end of the table.

Ace was almost grateful to Ernest for delaying the main course. She nudged the Doctor.

'What theories?' she whispered.

'Darwinism,' he replied. 'The theories that have set the whole of science in this country on its head.'

By now, Ernest was getting to his feet, a sanctimonious

smile on his face. Too late, Ace recognized the warning signs.

'Do we get a free lecture thrown in with dinner?' she muttered.

'Sermons are his speciality,' said the Doctor.

She giggled. 'Do we take notes?'

Before delivering any lecture, Ernest always felt it necessary to enlighten the less intelligent of his students with a few facts.

'Mr Smith disputes Man's rightful dominion over the forces over nature,' he began. But he had a less than rapt audience. Indeed Josiah was already ladling out servings of the calves' brains. Undeterred, Ernest raised his voice a tone and continued his condemnation. 'Instead, he says that mankind should itself adapt to serve nature or become extinct!'

He had thrown down his guantlet at last and he surveyed the table for the looks of outrage that would support his cause. Everyone else looked at Josiah.

Their host tensed for a moment and then slowly and deliberately laid aside his serving spoon. Ace could feel the malevolence as Josiah glared down the table at his opponent. She wanted the Doctor to intervene, to say something – anything – because in the dim gaslight, Josiah's black-lensed spectacles had given him the look of a death's head. She was certain that there were no depths to which this dusty, leech-like creature would not sink, and probably no horror that he was not capable of committing either. The loathsome Reverend Ernest Matthews faced him defiantly – a sitting target. Ace braced herself for something terrible.

'Well, sir . . .' growled Josiah. There was a sudden ring of a telephone from a room nearby. Josiah stopped abruptly; the ring came again. He glanced angrily at Mrs Pritchard, who gave a quick nod, then he rose apologizing to his guests and hurried from the dining room.

'Infernal telephonic machines,' complained Ernest, sinking back into his chair in disgust.

Gwendoline stared anxiously after her guardian; the

Doctor, deep in his thoughts, fiddled with his fish knife; the maids waited, positioned around the red walls like statues.

Ace couldn't bear the silence any longer. 'Let's ring out for a takeaway,' she suggested. 'Anyone fancy a curry?'

The Doctor folded his napkin and handed it to her.

'I know a nice little restaurant on the Khyber Pass,' he said.

He slipped out of his chair and followed Josiah. Ace would have gone after him but she couldn't leave Gwendoline at the mercy of Ernest Matthews. There could be few fates worse than being lectured to death and Ernest was already stirring in his chair.

'Where did you say this house was?' she asked quickly.

The telephone was still ringing when Josiah reached the study. He snatched up the earpiece and barked angrily into the device, 'Nimrod? What's going on? I told you not to call me during dinner.'

There was no response from the manservant, but Josiah could sense his presence listening.

'Nimrod! Are you there?'

'I . . . escape!' hissed a husky and genderless voice, a manifestation of loathing.

Josiah slammed down the earpiece as if it had burned him.

'It's learned to speak!' he choked.

More than that, however, it was loose. The unspeakable horror that had been locked away from his sight for so long had somehow released itself. No matter what had happened to Nimrod, the creature must be recaptured now – there was no telling what damage it could do. Josiah needed time to think, but his head was swimming. He reached out to ring for Mrs Pritchard.

'Having problems with your connections?' said a voice behind him.

The Doctor stood in the doorway; Josiah eyed him, uncertain of how much he knew or had heard. The Doctor came closer.

'Perhaps I can help,' he offered.

Josiah, however, was uncertain of the stranger's trustworthiness. The Doctor's whimsical smile was slightly mocking and his eyes betrayed an intelligence far keener than any Josiah had yet encountered. This was the only person that Josiah had not had to talk down to. He decided to take the Doctor into his confidence.

There was a distant yell from the hall. To his surprise, Josiah saw the Doctor's wilful composure crumple at the sound of Ace's summons.

'On the other hand,' the Doctor dithered, 'I think I have an emergency of my own. Please excuse me. Time to emerge.'

The Doctor hurried across the study to the other door and collided with Mrs Pritchard. He mumbled apologies as he disappeared from view. The housekeeper watched him go and then turned to her master.

'Mrs Pritchard, a problem has arisen,' said Josiah. 'Ask Ernest Matthews to join me in here.' He sounded unusually anxious.

'Very good, sir,' replied the housekeeper. She turned to go.

'And see to it that no one disturbs us.'

Mrs Pritchard gave a smile that might curdle milk or frighten puppies. Several curled petals fell from a bowl of chrysanthemums on the table. Mrs Pritchard nodded knowingly and closed the door behind her.

Ace was still in the hall yelling when the Doctor found her. She rounded on him, wild eyed.

'Face-ache Matthews in there says this house is called Gabriel Chase!'

'So?' he said quietly.

'You know why! Last time I saw it, it was all falling down. That was in 1983! You lied to me! This is Perivale!'

She was lost for things to say. She hadn't realized she could hate the Doctor so much. He tried to take her arm, but she pulled clear.

The doors of the drawing room opened. The Doctor

turned to look at the two emerging maids; Ace saw her chance and ran up the stairs away from him.

From her position in the drawing room, Gwendoline saw the Doctor dart up the staircase in pursuit of Ace. Then the maids closed the doors and she was alone.

How strange this evening was becoming, she thought. Sometimes trying to keep up with Uncle Josiah's games could make her feel quite giddy. She began to flick through the pile of sheet music on the piano until she found the song that she liked. She sat at the keyboard and began to play and sing.

'I don't know what it is about
My figure or my style,
But every time I walk abroad
The passers by all smile.
I lost myself in Kensington
About a week today.
I asked a cabby the way home
And to me he did say . . .'

The music echoed through the house as Mrs Pritchard admitted Ernest Matthews into Josiah's dimly lit study.

'Ernest, pray sit down,' said his host. Josiah genially indicated the armchair beside the fire, opposite his own.

Ernest sat down. He noticed that Mrs Pritchard was hovering beside Josiah's desk.

'I am afraid that something unforseen has arisen,' said Josiah. 'I regret I must ask you to wait a little longer.'

This was becoming tiresome, but Ernest Matthews, like a terrier, never let go once he had taken a bite.

'After coming so far sir, I have no intention of leaving until I have gained full satisfaction.'

'Then we are in accord,' smiled Josiah. 'Mrs Pritchard, see to it that the dean's time passes as quickly as possible.'

'Very good, sir.' Mrs Pritchard raised the handkerchief, into which she had just emptied half a bottle of chloroform, and smacked it full into Ernest's face.

As his mind swam into a tunnel of oblivion, Ernest heard

Gwendoline, his demurest of angels, embarking upon the jaunty chorus of her song.

> 'That's the way to the zoo,
> That's the way to the zoo.
> The moneky house is nearly full
> But there's room enough for you.
> Take a bus to Regent's Park,
> Make haste before it shuts.
> 'I'll come again on Monday
> And I'll bring you lots of nuts.'

Josiah regarded the unconscious Ernest, but his thoughts were elsewhere. If the escaped creature could learn to speak, then it might have learned to reason too. It could plot against him; it could smash everything that he, Josiah Samuel Smith, had worked for. Ridiculous! It was the basest of animals. It had simply learned to mimic human speech like a parrot.

'For the collection, sir?' enquired Mrs Pritchard, waiting patiently beside her victim.

'No, not yet,' said Josiah. His plans for the future would not be curtailed now. 'This specimen is for the toybox. I think he'll be most amusing.'

Nonetheless, Josiah had wasted too much time on Ernest Matthews. The creature had to be recaptured before it broke out into the house's open areas. The Doctor must be found too and his help enlisted. If he proved troublesome, then there was plenty of room in the toybox.

Desperate to be on her own, Ace had found her way back to the trophy room. Yet it wasn't easy to give the Doctor the slip: she heard him come in behind her and gently call her name but there was no way she was going to face him. She just kept thinking how he could do all this to her. She tried determinedly to keep her anger under control, but he was out of order and she had to say so.

'It's true, isn't it? This is the house I told you about,' she said.

He was right at her shoulder, speaking in her ear like a tempter, but she would not look at him. The piano tinkled mockingly away in the distance.

'When you were fourteen, you came over the wall for a dare,' said the Doctor.

'That's your surprise, isn't it? Bringing me back here. And it wasn't a dare!'

'Remind me what it was that you sensed when you got into the house. An aura of intense evil?'

What was this? she thought. Emotional therapy? He had gone far enough and she was going to turn the tables.

'Don't you have things you hate?'

The Doctor shrugged. 'I can't stand burnt toast and I loathe bus stations. They're nasty places, full of lost souls and lost luggage.'

'I told you I never wanted to come back here!'

'And then there's unrequited love,' he continued sadly, 'and tyranny and cruelty . . .'

'Too right!'

He began to edge round beside her. 'We each have a universe of our own terrors to face.'

She met his gaze head on. 'Then let me face them on my own terms!'

She turned away again and tried to concentrate on a display of neatly labelled crustacean shells. There was nothing else to say. Why couldn't he leave her alone?

'Don't tell me you didn't want to know what happened to this house?' he persisted.

'No!'

'But you've already learned something that you'd never have recognized when you were fourteen.'

'Like what?'

'The nature of the horror you sensed here in a hundred years' time.'

She knew he was right . . . as usual. And she had known the answer too if only she had stopped to think about it. Somehow it was always worse when it was on Earth.

'It's alien,' she said and the thought filled her with foreboding.

He touched her arm and asked her to come back to dinner. Ace didn't say a word. The Doctor sighed. Ace heard him moving away. It was no good, she had to tell him.

'When I lived here in Perivale, me and my best mate, we dossed around together. We'd out-dare each other on things – skiving off, stupid things. Then they burnt out Manisha's flat: white kids firebombed it and I didn't care any more.'

The piano had stopped and it was so quiet Ace thought that the Doctor had gone.

'I think that you really cared a lot, Ace,' said his voice right beside her again.

'That's when I got into the house – this house. I was so mad and I needed to get away. The place was empty, all overgrown and falling down. No one came here.'

She stopped and looked round at the walls, where the heads of the dead wild creatures stared blank-eyed down at her.

'But when I got inside, it was even worse.'

She could feel it again now, the whole thing pressing in around her.

'I didn't know then . . . It was horrible.'

There was so much she wanted to say, things that should have come out years ago. At last she could exorcise it once and for all.

'What did you do, Ace?' he insisted.

'Doctor? I must speak with you,' said Josiah.

Ace saw him standing in the doorway and stopped talking.

'Tell me, Ace!' demanded the Doctor, trying to motion the intruder away.

Ace panicked and ran. She barged past the sepulchral figure, who quickly closed the door behind her and stepped into the frustrated Doctor's path.

'I need your help, Doctor,' he said.

Then get in the queue, thought the Doctor. But he knew that Ace would have to wait. He hoped she would not get into any more trouble.

The Doctor stepped back from the door and walked

around the workbench with its monkey skeleton. Because Josiah and he were plainly going to talk business, he decided not to pull any punches.

'It can't be easy being so far away from home,' said the Doctor, 'struggling to adapt to an alien environment.'

Josiah somehow managed to look totally surprised; the Doctor was impressed.

'My roots are in this house,' he declared. 'I'm as human as you are.'

'Yes,' said the Doctor

A look of hatred came over Josiah's wizened face. 'How you fancy people despise me,' he said, 'with your doctorates and your professorships.'

The Doctor rested one elbow on the workbench, cupped his chin in his hand and watched Josiah go through his territorial displays.

'Honours aren't everything,' he observed.

'I am afflicted with an enemy,' said Josiah. 'A vile and base creature pitted against me, that I am forced to serve. All of us in this house are in its power.'

He produced a large white bank-note from his pocket. Unfolding the note he insinuated in the Doctor's direction. 'I believe you can assist me in defeating it.'

'I'm not interested in money,' said the Doctor. 'How much?' he added, just out of curiosity.

'Five thousand pounds to rid me of the evil brute.'

The Doctor whistled. 'Now that's what I call Victorian value,' he teased. 'But I'm still not interested in money.' Five thousand pounds! he thought. A gentleman only ever pays in guineas!

Josiah was used to having his own way. He screwed up the bank-note in his gloved fist; he crushed anything that opposed him.

The Doctor sauntered out of the room, busily turning over the new information in his mind. Perhaps Josiah really did believe himself to be human and there must be a few grains of truth in the rest of what he had said. The Doctor decided to humour Josiah to see how desperate he got. But he had to keep Ace out of trouble.

★ ⋆★ ★

Ace had come back down the stairs without knowing where she was going. From the hall, she could hear sounds from the drawing room and the staff moving deeper in the house. What did she come down here for? She didn't want to see anyone. There was no point going outside into the night. She should have gone up to the top of the house, out of the way, where the TARDIS was.

She turned to go back up the staircase but she could hear more movement from above. There seemed to be nowhere to hide, until she noticed a set of panelled doors at the far side of the hall.

She went closer and saw that they must be the entrance to a lift which would take her up through the house unhindered. Quickly opening the doors, she entered the red velvet interior. Closing the doors, she slid the folding metal gate shut, turned the brass lever on the wall and looked up expectantly. With a clunk, the mechanism engaged and the lift went down through the floor.

Mrs Pritchard had been observing Ace for some time from behind a tall, potted palm. She emerged from her hiding place and crossed to the lift doors. She stood listening to the machinery clanking as the lift descended through the solid bedrock deep beneath the house.

Her master was a fool if he imagined she did not know what went on in her house. If the creature had escaped, then sending it the Doctor's brat was one way of forestalling it. Besides, it had not been fed yet tonight, so that might solve one more problem.

She heard the distant clang of the lift as it stopped. She waited, however, with her finger poised over the panel of buttons on the wall.

Ace was already frightened by the long and unexpected descent. Her ears had kept popping as the lift went deeper and deeper until she began to think it would never stop. She tried the lever on the lift wall, but it refused to move. Warily sliding back the lift gate, she opened the doors and peered out into the gloomy tunnel. She could hear water dripping, but the air was fresher than she expected and there was a glow coming from the far end. She had only dared to take a few paces along the tunnel before she froze stock still. She was certain she had heard something scuttling up ahead.

The lift gate immediately clattered shut behind her and the doors slammed tightly closed. Ace clawed at the handle, but it had been secured from the inside.

In the hall above, Mrs Pritchard pressed a second button. She smiled grimly as she heard the lift commence its upward journey; she knew it would be empty when it reached the top.

7

Ace's Adventures Underground

There was nowhere to go except down the tunnel. Ace could make out shapes and patterns on the curved walls as she edged nearer to the hazy glow. The pictures were reminiscent of prehistoric cave paintings: there were matchstick hunters, a bison, mammoths and a bear. At the centre was a white splash that could have been fire or the sun – it was some sort of light anyway, because all the figures around it had the side of them closest to the splash painted in white as if they were reflecting the glow.

Ace hadn't developed her faculties as an art critic much beyond saying 'Wow!' when she saw something she really liked, but she could see that the hunting pictures were more refined than the average palaeolithic mural. The paint was fresh too. Nimrod had come a long way from finger painting and scratching walls with old bones and burnt sticks.

Ace moved along to the tunnel mouth. It was like stepping through a veil as she entered the chamber. There was a cry like a startled bird as the slight haze closed behind her. The stuffed birds and antique furniture were no surprise to her, but the vaulted ceiling whose lines descended through the carved, buttressed walls and the flickering screens and glittering clusters of crystals made her think of Aladdin's cave. It was either immensely advanced or incredibly archaic. The place was timeless, as if it had always been there; perhaps it had even carved itself.

At the heart of the chamber pulsed a glowing membrane, radiating its energies from the wall where it was set.

'Wow!' said Ace, but she knew that this was where all the trouble came from. She could see the shadow stirring on the surface of the membrane. The pulse was starting to boom into her head and scare the hell out of her.

There was a dark shape on the floor near to the membrane. Nimrod still lay senseless where he had fallen, beside a silver-topped gentleman's cane. Ace could see a dull bruise through the coarse hair on his neck. As she bent over him, she felt that she was being watched.

The curtain that covered the alcove across the chamber slowly drew open to disclose the tableau of two Victorian gentlemen in dusty evening attire. The heads of both figures were bloated and grey, dried and flaking like the sloughed skins of creatures which had long outgrown these bodies.

One was an insect, its huge eyes bulging at the sides of its hairy head and sharp mandibles extruding from its mouth. Instead of hands, serrated pincers protruded from its gold-linked cuffs.

The other figure's head was reptilian, but its chameleon eyes were set low down, almost at the wattles on its throat. There seemed to be no mouth on its gnarled head, but its hands must have been humanoid because they were encased in white kid-gloves. This must be another of Josiah's displays, and it was the most repulsive so far.

There was a hiss from close by. The heavy door set in the granite buttress creaked back and forth in its portal. For a second, the eye watching through the spyhole met directly with Ace's own stare.

The girl shuddered and started to back away. Was this the terror she had felt before? And would it still be waiting for her in the house's future, the future which was her past? It was starting all over again. She was going to get trapped in a loop of time, endlessly travelling through the same events on a Möbius strip of her own making. And that thing would always be watching her for ever.

The door stayed closed, but it creaked to and fro,

mocking her fear. Then the voice came, rough and half-growled like an animal learning to talk.

'There's a new scent in the dark. Listen! Pulsing, warming, racing blood. Smells like Ratkin!'

One eye in the reptile husk's head swivelled towards Ace. Both figures in the tableau began to twitch and sway.

'Go on!' ordered the voice. 'Move yourselves! Move! Ratkin's come to visit!'

Slowly, step by shuffled step, the husks moved forward towards Ace. She heard the fluttering of wings in her head. The frozen birds shrieked all around her, the energy pulsed and the voice chanted, 'Move! Move! Move!'

'Doctor!' yelled Ace. She scrambled for the tunnel. The reptilian husk opened the flaplike mouth on the top of its head and bellowed. The insect chittered its response.

'Fetch!' urged the voice.

The two creatures staggered forward like tangled puppets in pursuit of their prey.

Through the eyes of the reptilian husk, the creature saw Ratkin struggling with the doors to the lift. 'Trap's biting shut, Ratkin! No way up!'

The creature wanted Ratkin to squeal as the husks closed in, but it just kicked and squirmed.

'You don't frighten me!' it yelped as the husks reached for it. It called 'Doctor!' again as they grasped Ratkin and dragged it back towards the chamber.

'Fetch closer,' ordered the voice as the husks approached the door.

The insect husk's pincers cut into Ace's arm, forcing her to give up her struggle. 'What do you want?' she yelled at the watching eye.

The voice mocked her without mercy. 'No escaping, Ratkin! No way up. No hoping!'

'You don't have to hide in there,' she retaliated. 'You've got me. You can come out now. I dare you!'

There was a pitiful whine which deepened into a snarl. Ace tried to pull back but was held fast as the door swung outward to reveal the darkness inside the cell.

A half-lit shape covered in filthy rags slowly emerged

76

from the shadows. Suddenly a figure darted in front of Ace and slammed the door shut. The trapped creature screamed with rage as Nimrod jammed the bolt back into position. With the will that animated them momentarily broken, the husks slackened their grip allowing Ace to pull free.

The door shook under a battery of blows from inside. 'Are you hurt, miss?' asked Nimrod.

'I'll survive,' she said. 'What is that thing in there?'

The trapped creature had fallen silent. Nimrod, apparently no worse for wear from his attack, regarded the cell door.

The voice inside hissed out again, 'My freeness! Open door!' and the husks lurched back into life to obey.

Nimrod pulled Ace clear of their path. There was a hurricane lamp on the floor, used on the occasions when he cleared out the creature's cell. A device of Josiah's modification, it lit at the touch of a button. Nimrod seized hold of the lamp now and swung the glowing light source into the husks' faces.

Slowly driven back, the husks bellowed in fear. The voice continued to shriek its ineffectual orders. Ace clung close to Nimrod as they tried to force a way towards the tunnel.

'They don't like the light, do they?' she yelled over the racket.

Nimrod gave her the strangest look and the voice, as if it had heard, snarled out a new instruction. 'Destroy lamp!'

The reptilian husk lunged at the lantern, knocking it from Nimrod's hand to the floor where it shattered.

'I'll sort you lot out!' shouted Ace. She grabbed the silver cane from the floor and began to swing it in front of her.

Nimrod grasped her arm, pulling her backwards into the gap between the crystal console and the pulsing membrane on the wall.

'Round here,' he said. 'They won't dare come near the core.'

'Why? What are they scared of?' Ace was spoiling for a fight. Use the resources available; that's what the Doctor always does.

'Oi, you in there!' she called to the cell door. 'What's it worth not to smash the place up?'

'No!' whispered Nimrod, shaking his head. 'You don't know what you're doing.'

But Ace's approach was working; the husks had stopped moving. Ace raised the cane and held it close to the membrane.

'Call them off or I'll start with this!' she shouted.

Ace saw the eye at the spyhole widen in shock.

'No!' howled the creature. 'Hide me!'

The husks started to stagger backwards to form a shield in front of the door.

Nimrod leaned over to snatch the cane from Ace's grasp, but she dodged clear, still keeping close to the membrane.

'I mean it, Tarzan, I'll do it!' she warned.

'No letting it out!' wailed the voice behind the door. 'Light burning with angriness!'

Nimrod could see the shadow behind the membrane beginning to stir. He tried to stay calm and reached out again for the cane.

'Give it to me,' he begged. 'You are profaning the Temple of Light.'

'I'll profane you in a minute!' she retaliated. She had got this far without the Doctor and she wasn't going back now. The thing behind the door was still wailing; it was getting on her nerves.

'And shut that thing up too!'

Nimrod edged towards Ace, but she saw him and brought the cane up between them. He tried to reason with her.

'You are afraid and do not understand, miss. The Burning One must not be woken!'

He grabbed hold of the cane and tried to wrest it from her. Ace would have given back as good as she got, but the Neanderthal was much too strong. She lost her footing and they both toppled sideways, crunching against the brittle surface of the membrane. Energy exploded out and danced around them, hurling Ace and Nimrod to the floor; the whole chamber shuddered as jets of steam like the outlets of giant pistons hissed from vents in the stone buttresses.

Behind the door, the creature howled and remembered its name. It was Control and there was no escape!

The Doctor had spent some time acquainting himself with the layout of the house while avoiding the maids in the process. His main task was to find Ace, but she had not returned to the TARDIS as he had expected. As he came back down from the observatory, he had to dodge a group of maids carrying something of extreme bulk up the narrow spiral staircase. He hid behind a stuffed white peacock, whose fan of tail feathers obscured his view, leaving him none the wiser about the nature of the maids' burden.

Behind a locked door on the second level, he heard Redvers Fenn-Cooper deep in conversation with himself. 'They gave Redvers a bed, but he's slept on the bare ground since he was a boy . . . under the stars, huh, under the trees . . . under canvas, under the bed.'

The Doctor smiled. He thought it was a fortunate man who could choose his own friends.

On the first floor, he overheard Josiah conversing with Mrs Pritchard in the trophy room. They were cataloguing the stock of breech-loaders and pistols needed for their expedition. Mrs Pritchard affirmed that she did not expect her staff to perform any task that she was not prepared to undertake herself. Josiah laughed in gratification.

When he reached the ground floor, the Doctor steered clear of the drawing and dining rooms for fear of another encounter with Ernest Matthews. Instead, he slipped into Josiah's study.

As he rifled through the contents of the desk, he noticed a sturdy, gentleman's walking shoe lying discarded on the floor.

'If found, please return to the Reverend Ernest Matthews, Mortarhouse College, Oxford,' he muttered as he examined the shoe.

There was a sudden click. The Doctor darted for cover behind the door as Gwendoline entered, still dressed in her dinner-jacket. At first the Doctor thought she was sleep-walking, for she almost glided across the room with a dreamy expression on her face.

Gwendoline knelt before a large chest of drawers and opened the top drawer. She revealed a tray of exquisitely coloured tropical butterflies, each one mounted on card. After staring at them for a moment, she slid the drawer back into place and drew out the next one.

The Doctor moved stealthily out of hiding to observe ranks of mounted beetles, cockchafers and scorpions shining in their polished armour.

Gwendoline closed the drawer again and began to pull out the third and deepest compartment. As it slid out, the Doctor grimly surveyed the contents. It was somehow inevitable that Josiah's collection of fauna should encompass human beings as well.

'Butterflies, beetles . . . and bluebottles,' he remarked aloud.

Gwendoline was unsurprised by his presence. She sat on the floor and smiled at the perfectly preserved specimen of a Victorian inspector of police. He lay in the drawer in his full dress uniform with his cape spread and pinned out like wings.

'I think it's my favourite in the whole collection,' she said. 'It's all the way from Java.'

'Java?' asked the Doctor. He carelessly dangled the shoe from one finger.

Gwendoline hardly seemed to notice, although she nervously fingered her locket chain.

'The Reverend Ernest Matthews will be leaving for Java soon,' she said. 'Perhaps he will see my father.'

'Your father? Is he in Java too?'

Gwendoline took the shoe from the Doctor and studied it curiously. 'Uncle Josiah sent him there because of what he saw in the cellar.' She smiled sweetly. 'I suppose it must be the fashion.'

The Doctor took a deep breath. 'Gwendoline, do you know where Ace is? Only she can be rather explosive when her temper's up.'

The girl's attention had returned to the policeman in the drawer. 'It's so lovely,' she said. 'The way its wings catch the light.'

'What's in the cellar, Gwendoline?' said the Doctor, firmly taking her arm.

She looked round at him, a picture of wide-eyed innocence, and said, 'I do hope Ace hasn't gone to Java yet.'

He scowled. 'How convenient – only seeing what Uncle Josiah wants you to see.'

Gwendoline showed no sign of interest in this remark at all.

'Frankly,' he continued, snapping his fingers angrily in her face, 'you wouldn't notice the Albert Memorial if it landed on your foot. And if anything's happened to Ace, I'll drop it on your head!'

He stalked angrily out of the study. Selective hypnosis was just the sort of crude device the Doctor had expected from Josiah. It was typical of the contempt in which Josiah held the humans he treated so cruelly as playthings.

Gwendoline was startled out of her reverie as the study door slammed. She quickly closed the drawer and hurried after the Doctor.

As he walked into the hall, the Doctor saw the group of maids waiting in ranks beside the pair of gates, which he assumed belonged to a lift. Mrs Pritchard was with the maids but there was no sign of Ace. The housekeeper laid aside her hunting rifle and fixed the Doctor with her eyes. Her advance on the Doctor, however, was curtailed by a voice from the staircase above.

'So there you are, Doctor. Have you considered my offer?'

The Doctor looked up at Josiah, who was descending to meet them.

'To murder your enemy?' I'm not your pet executioner,' he snapped. 'Where's Ace?'

Josiah's grin vanished into a threatening glare. 'Be careful, Doctor. To cross me would be a serious error.'

Mrs Pritchard had closed in and was indicating the stair with all the charm of a smiling snake. 'Miss Ace has already retired to bed, sir,' she crooned. 'Come and I will show you.'

The Doctor turned away from the unctuous apparition

and was face to face with Gwendoline, who stepped up with a lit candle.

'Here, Doctor, to light you to bed,' she said. In lullaby tones she added, 'Sleep well. Good night.'

'Good night. Sleep tight. Up the wooden hill to Bedford-shire, otherwise known as Java!' the Doctor chanted angrily, trapped between two assailants. 'Well, not tonight, Josiaphine!'

He blew out the candle and broke free, heading towards the lift.

'Your puppet show doesn't fool me. Sorry to ruin your big hunt, but Ace is in trouble. She's down this way I take it,' he said, indicating the lift beyond the maids.

With one concerted movement, the servants turned and aimed their pistols at his head.

'Five thousand pounds to lead this rabble?' sniffed the Doctor. He turned to look at Josiah, at the blue veins pumping beneath the flaking, bleached skin of his temples. 'You'd do better to spend it on a few lessons in etiquette. And a clean jacket!'

With a sharp intake of breath, Josiah drew back his hand to strike the Doctor, but he was stopped by a tremor which ran up through the house and rattled its fitments. Josiah, with a look of sudden fear, spun back to gaze up at the window above the stairs. A moment later, the stained glass began to hum and flare with patterns of light.

'What's it done?' he cried, clutching at the banister to steady himself. 'It'll destroy us all!'

The maids stared round in confusion, desperately searching for instruction.

The Doctor seized his chance, pulled the Geiger counter from his pocket and held it to Josiah's head. Dragging his prisoner back towards the gates, he yelled, 'Get the lift!'

Mrs Pritchard nodded and one of the maids scrambled to obey.

With Josiah inside, the Doctor snapped shut the gate and grasped the lever. 'Right, Josiah, let's see what's down the rabbit hole,' he said. He pushed the mechanism into gear; the lift shuddered and began to clank downwards.

The Doctor had expected a torrent of abuse, but Josiah only stared at the rock walls of the lift shaft as they passed. Deciding to let him stew, the Doctor concentrated on estimating their speed and the depth of their descent.

A dread of what awaited them at the foot of the shaft preyed on Josiah's thoughts. If his worst fears were realized, then this meddlesome Doctor who was holding a weapon to his head was the least of his worries. All his work – everything he had achieved alone – could be swept away in a single gesture of burning tumult. But would it come to that? There was no word from Nimrod, but there were no further threats from the escaped creature until this sudden disturbance. Base as it was, the creature must be subject to the same instincts as all living animals. Surely fear would prevent it from disturbing the core. Pray that it was so. Yet there were other possibilities too: if the Doctor's brat of a companion had already discovered the secret chamber, there was no knowing what harm she might do, or what fate might befall her.

Josiah's work had endured many insults and rebuttals, but he would not relinquish everything for which he had striven. His research had taken him further than any other published scientist. He would achieve his aim to catalogue every variety of living creature on the planet. Yet they sneered at him and refused to admit a newcomer through the portals of their societies and gentlemen's clubs.

It was the fate of any great innovator to be misunderstood and ridiculed; he was no exception. He had no blood lineage, neither had he been to the right school. He was an outsider, condemned to stare through the steamy window of Victorian respectability. But if there was a future, they would learn to change their attitudes just as it was in him to change, chameleon-like, to teach them who was dominant. Let them all mock, but he would not be alienated!

The lift jolted to a halt. The Doctor slid back the gate and directed Josiah out with the Geiger counter. From the far end of the passage came a tremulous pulse of sound and a glow made almost tangible by the mist that hovered there.

Josiah clutched at the wall in fear. 'Light!' he choked.

'. . . at the end of the tunnel,' added the Doctor.

He paused to examine the paintings on the curved walls. The brushwork was fine and detailed, even nineteenth century gothic in style.

'Palaeolithic cave paintings,' he mused, 'but done in oils. Nimrod must be getting homesick.'

The Doctor urged Josiah further on until they reached the veil of light that marked the entrance to the inner chamber.

From the outside, the Doctor could make out the contours of the chamber which was lit by flickering screens whose shifting patterns coloured the mist blue to green to gold. The walls groaned their protest as vents around the chamber jetted steam into the area. At its heart, from which all its power stemmed, the giant oval membrane throbbed with piercing luminescence.

Josiah held back at the mouth of the passage. He was close to panic and taking short gulps of air. He warily eyed the scene until the Doctor pushed him into the centre. The penetrated veil emitted its shrill cry, either of alarm or acknowledgement, and it was like standing in the heart of a living jewel. Colour and light shimmered and darted around Josiah and the Doctor, it silhouetted the figure that rose from beside the membrane and moved towards them.

Ace flung her arms around the Doctor and demanded to know where he had been.

'Where haven't I been?' he replied, slightly embarrassed at this show of affection in front of his prisoner. 'I came as quick as I could,' he added brusquely.

Josiah ignored the Doctor's gun and rounded on Ace. 'What have you done to my observatory?' he accused.

'It's what it nearly did to me!' she retorted.

The Doctor glanced around the chamber, taking in the Victorian furnishings in their archaic surroundings. Through the hissing jets of steam he could see two motionless shapes standing hunched by the closed door of a cell and a figure that knelt before the huge membrane and stared deep into its glowing heart at the shadow that stirred there.

The Doctor turned sternly back to his protégée and said, 'Ace? Have you been tampering?'

'It was an accident!' she protested.

Josiah was not slow to shift the blame and attention from his own shoulders. 'All my work could be ruined!' he declared.

'That's my girl,' the Doctor said proudly. He handed her the Geiger counter.

Ace studied it for a second before the Doctor removed it from her grasp, turned it round, gave it back and directed her aim towards Josiah.

'Keep him covered,' said the Doctor before he sauntered across the chamber towards the figure that knelt beside the membrane.

One of the jets of steam spurted out and almost caught the Doctor in the face. He scooped up a brass waste-paper basket from the floor, caught the jet in it and plugged the basket over the vent on the wall.

'Not a patch on the Flying Scotsman,' he muttered, dusting off his hands and flicking at an outcrop of crystals beside the vent.

Josiah watched as the steam jets died around the chamber. The Doctor was interfering with his property and he was powerless to stop it. He must find out the extent of the damage. He looked back at the girl as she aimed the gun squarely at his head, and noticed how the flickering instrumentation on the weapon altered as the energetic activity in the chamber subsided.

'Don't try anything,' Ace said fiercely.

Shielding his eyes against the glare, Josiah saw the Doctor bending over the figure by the membrane. The shadow was still shifting uneasily inside; he had to act now.

'Nimrod!' he shouted. 'Get up you fool! It's got to be stopped!'

The Doctor snapped his fingers a couple of times under the entranced Neanderthal's nose. When he got no response, the Doctor placed his hands on the sides of Nimrod's temples.

'Best not to move him,' he advised.

'He fell against that,' said Ace, pointing to the membrane with the Geiger counter.

'And disturbed whatever's hibernating inside,' the Doctor concluded, reaching forward to examine the cracks in the membrane's crust through which light was seeping.

'Don't touch it!' yelled Josiah, who suddenly found himself staring back down the muzzle of Ace's gun.

'You're scared of it too, just like the others,' she said.

'Because he knows what it is. Don't you, Josiah?' added the Doctor. 'No one builds an observatory this deep. You can't see many stars down here.'

Josiah was beginning to breathe unsteadily again. 'There's an energy escape,' he pleaded. 'I must stabilize it!'

The Doctor was making his way across the chamber towards the two shapes by the cell door. 'Don't worry. I always leave things until the last minute,' he said, peering at the inanimate monstrosities in their formal evening dress. 'These husks: they're some of your old cast-offs, I take it?'

'They attacked me and Nimrod,' said Ace.

The Doctor smiled. 'You couldn't have been introduced properly.'

'You're insane!' shouted Josiah. 'If the membrane is broken . . .'

'Yes?' said the Doctor, but Josiah just scowled and fell silent.

'There's something well vicious behind that door too that's controlling the husks,' added Ace.

The Doctor approached the cell door and looked in at the spyhole.

'Vicious, like most maltreated caged animals,' he said.

It was pitch black inside and it smelled unpleasantly of uncleaned stables. The bolt was not closed. In the darkness, he could hear something breathing gently. Perhaps it would be better to slide the bolt home.

'Yeah, but even that bottled out when I threatened to smash the membrane,' boasted Ace.

'You did what!' hissed Josiah.

'Ace!' The Doctor spun round from the door and the girl

86

looked down shamefaced at the floor, embarrassed by the carelessness of her admission.

The Doctor smiied at Josiah and walked across to the desk at the centre of the chamber.

'Sounds like a fine kettle of fish all set to boil over,' he observed. Whether by accident or design he rested his hand on the brass buttons on the desk top.

The whole chamber groaned as the screens set in its walls flared into life. Ace saw unknown figures and shapes spinning across their surfaces. Indeed, the haze of the chamber seemed to draw the patterns swirling out into the air before them. Forgetting her prisoner, Ace crossed the chamber to stare fascinated beside the Doctor.

'Genetic codes, DNA, RNA and chromosome indices,' he observed. 'You've done a lot of exploring down here, haven't you, Josiah?' he added, still engrossed.

Suddenly – at last, the Doctor would have thought – Ace understood what she was looking at.

'It's a stone spaceship!' she cried.

'Hmm,' concurred the Doctor, 'and the owner won't be too happy when it wakes up.'

'I am the owner,' insisted Josiah's voice from behind them.

The Doctor's solution was triumphant.

'No, you're not. You're just part of the cargo.'

He spun on his heel and saw Josiah aiming a pistol which he had just extracted froom the desk drawer at them.

'You're so smug and self-satisfied, Doctor,' he sneered.

'I try,' the Doctor said quietly.

Ace brought the Geiger counter up in answer to the pistol.

'Drop it,' she ordered.

Josiah shook his head.

'I'm not a simpleton. And that device is a radiation detector, not a gun.'

Using the pistol, he directed them towards the crystalline console in front of the membrane.

'You're going to help me stabilize the energy loss, or most of southern England goes up in the firestorm.'

The shadow in the core had begun to stir again; plumes of steam trickled from the vents. Around them, the stone walls of the ship growled their protest as the symbols danced off the screens into the miasma.

The terrified Control creature watched its enemy and his prisoners from the spyhole. Like a balance of scales, the links between the two could not be broken, even as the distance between them grew ever further apart. The Control creature sensed the growing feeling of isolation and loneliness. It also felt strange and had done ever since the day when, in the depths of its despairing misery, it found it had shed its tail. As Control struggled to understand, it felt only hatred for the one who had become Josiah and from whom it could never escape. But far more than Josiah, it feared the anger of the power they both served: the fulcrum on which both their lives were balanced. If it was woken, they would all burn in the fury of Light. Control clawed at the door from the inside; the prison was open, but the creature was too frightened to go out.

The glare from the membrane became fiercer as the Doctor and Ace took their places beside the crystal slab. Keeping his distance behind the safety of the gun, Josiah ordered them to drive the extended crystal rods into the console on his instruction.

Squinting across the console from the intensity of the glow, Ace confided, 'After this I'll get a job at Sellafield. It'll be safer.'

'Just do what I do when I do it,' muttered the Doctor.

'Very helpful,' she grumbled.

'Lower the first rod,' instructed Josiah, but the Doctor was having none of it.

'Oh dear, oh dear,' he began like a front-of-curtain, music-hall comic, 'skeletons in the cupboard, husks in the cellar . . .'

'Bats in the belfry!' chimed in Ace.

Josiah raised his gun as the rumbling of the ship grew louder.

'Just do it!' he snarled.

'Now, now,' quipped the Doctor. 'You'll never evolve into a nice Victorian gentleman if you shout.'

Ace glanced at the figures by the cell door. 'Did those husks really used to be him?' she asked. 'And I thought my family were trouble.'

You should see mine, the Doctor was about to say, but he thought better of it and added, 'That's right. Not much improvement on the reptile, is he?'

'I said now!' yelled Josiah, taking several steps forward.

'Now!' shouted the Doctor and rammed as many of the rods into the slab as he could manage at one go.

Ace followed suit as the Doctor turned and pulled the bronze waste-paper basket from its steam vent on the wall. The ship roared as a jet of vapour spurted out and caught Josiah full in the face. He stumbled back with a scream, his hands to his eyes and fell to the floor, where he lay scrabbling in the glare for his dropped spectacles.

Ace kicked the gun out of reach as he lunged for it.

'Nice try,' she grinned.

For a second she saw his uncovered eyes. Veinless white globes with black spot pupils and no irises stared at her with inhuman loathing.

As the roar of the angry ship subsided into its steady regular pulse, Josiah's eyes seemed to flicker with palest blue. The glare from the screens and membrane dulled into the faintest glow and Josiah rose unsteadily to recover his composure and face his enemies.

'I think congratulations are in order,' said the Doctor expectantly.

'Congratulations,' said Ace, just as she caught the first twitching movements of the husks. 'Maybe not . . .' she added as the door to the cell began to creak slowly open. 'Professor! Here we go again!'

Josiah cried out and began to stumble towards the tunnel and the lift. The husks bellowed and chattered Control's anger as they staggered forward. The Doctor grabbed the still transfixed Nimrod and, with Ace's help, dragged the manservant after Josiah.

Through the eyes of the flailing husks, Control saw its

chance of escape vanishing. Relinquishing its driving will over them, it darted from its cell. Control's flying grey rags made it look like a monstrous bride in pursuit of an absconding lover.

The Doctor caught the door as Josiah tried to slide it closed against him. He and Ace bundled the unconscious Nimrod inside the plush compartment and Josiah, seeing the approaching shape, forced the metal gate across.

There was a scream as Control snatched at the closing gap and thrust a filthy, gloved claw into the cramped interior of the lift.

'Give me my freeness!' snarled its voice, as the claw lashed the air only inches from the lift's occupants.

Josiah, his eyes full of terror, hurled all his weight at the door; Ace joined him. To her horror, she saw the Doctor reach out and delicately take the tips of the claws and shake them gently.

'How do you do?' he said. 'I'm the Doctor and this is . . .'

'Just call me Ratkin!' Ace butted in angrily.

She pulled back sharply as the claws groped at the Doctor's jacket and wrenched at his tie, half choking him in the process.

The creature had begun to whine pathetically, 'Poor Control. No way up. No escaping. No hoping.'

'Don't listen to it!' hissed Josiah, using all his weight to keep the door closed. 'It's a depraved monstrosity!'

'Depraved or deprived?' snapped the Doctor. He grabbed at the creature's arm and indulgently stroked the top of the struggling claw in a vain attempt to free himself.

'There, there. There's a poor Control.' He looked from the arm to Josiah and back to the arm again. 'Now, which of you is Jekyll and which one Hyde?' he asked.

At once, Control's voice grew pitiful as it whimpered, 'Spare a farthing, guv'nor. Pity poor Control. Locked away. All on lone.'

'Fiend!' roared Josiah and slammed his fist into the claw, which withdrew with an accompanying shriek. The door slammed shut and he twisted the lever home.

90

As the lift trundled upwards and Control's howls of rage receded beneath them, Josiah fell to the floor in a swoon and lay trembling feverishly beside Nimrod. The Doctor leaned over Josiah and saw how the bleached, white skin on his head was flaking and turning translucent grey. The white hair had become brittle and crumbled to the touch.

'Is he dying?' Ace asked wearily, unwilling to admit that she was also almost too exhausted to stand up.

'He's had a hard day's night,' diagnosed the Doctor. 'He's evolving again . . . into his next stage.'

It might take other life forms thousands of years, but Josiah was able to change his physical form before their very eyes. Ace shuddered at the thought, but the Doctor sat cross-legged on the floor and pondered silently, awaiting new developments in whatever form they might evolve.

8

Creature Comforts

Dinner had been served late that evening and it had been well into the early hours before Josiah and the Doctor had made their descent in the lift. Deprived of her master, Mrs Pritchard understood that her duty was to wait as long as was necessary until he returned. She stationed her maids beside the lift gates and stood immobile at their head, staring at the slow progress of the clock.

Distant thunder rumbled occasionally. It came not from the clear sky, which was bright with stars, but echoed in the ground on which the house stood.

At close on half past three o'clock, she was suddenly aware of a strange whimpering sound from close by. She turned to seek out the source of this annoyance and discovered Gwendoline still dressed in a gentleman's dinner-jacket, sitting on the stairs and blubbing into her bare hands.

The maids began to cluster behind their mistress, staring coldly at the snivelling creature.

Gwendoline turned her red-rimmed eyes up to the house-keeper, twisted her locket in her hands and blurted through the tears, 'Why did father go to Java and leave me?' And where is my mother? I try and try, but I cannot understand.'

There was no sympathy to be had from the servants. Mrs Pritchard responded with a harshness more fitting to a governess than a member of the domestic staff.

'That is a wicked thing to say. Wicked! Your mother would be ashamed could she but hear you. Sitting there dressed like a music-hall trollop! It's this Doctor filling your head with ideas.'

'His words are so confusing,' confessed Gwendoline. She rose to her feet and wiped her eyes with Ace's tissue. 'Uncle Josiah's ideas are much easier to understand.' With a sudden sense of purpose, she determinedly undid the bow tie at her collar.

'Go upstairs and dress yourself properly,' advised the housekeeper.

Gwendoline instinctively moved to obey her servant's instruction, but half-way up the stairs she halted and looked back. Mrs Pritchard was staring up at her with a puzzled frown. For one moment, Gwendoline was tempted to treat this as insolence but the housekeeper immediately looked away and resumed her place at the head of her staff. The clock chimed the half hour and Gwendoline made her way back to her room.

Things made sense as long as she thought of Uncle Josiah. Thus she found herself putting on a dress of dusky blue, because it suited her mood and that of the house too – it was full of secret desires and unknown gestures. There were some that Uncle Josiah shared with her, and if she was good he might share more. But there in her room, among the familiar bric-à-brac, was the broken bird toy and the strange clothes that Ace had left behind when they had changed for dinner.

She examined the glossy material of the jacket. It felt unnatural and slippery. Of the coloured medals and badges that adorned it, the letters BSA made no sense to her, nor did Ace Roofing Co. Her ideas were becoming muddled again. Was it Ace or Alice? Sometimes she could hardly remember if it was day or night. Her guardian always became fearfully angry when she asked questions, but she needed to talk to someone.

Before she knew it, she was outside the room where Mr Fenn-Cooper was being cared for. He was certainly that, for when she opened the door he was lying on his side in a pool of moonlight, snugly wrapped in his strait-jacket. She heard him say 'Not much time left. It'll soon be light,' before he noticed she was there and fell silent.

When she called his name, he looked startled and said, 'So you've seen Redvers too. I knew he was close by. Where are they holding the poor devil?'

'I am lost, so lost and alone,' she pleaded, close to tears again.

The explorer managed to sit up in the presence of his young visitor. 'Redvers understands. He got used to loneliness in the bush,' he sympathized, but Gwendoline was becoming desperate.

'I cannot find my mother,' she blurted. 'I'm sure she was here.'

With some difficulty, Redvers scrambled to his feet. 'Don't be alarmed,' he advised. Even in his bonds, he presented a formidable figure that towered above Gwendoline. She backed away in fear.

Redvers struggled inside the strait-jacket, unable to break free. 'Redvers always escapes in the end,' he muttered and began to advance on the shrinking girl. 'He knows where the greatest secret of all is hidden. It sleeps in the depths of the interior. And it must never be woken!'

He made a sudden move forward, but Gwendoline was there before him. She darted into the passage and shut the door, quickly turning the key in the lock. The problem with asking questions was that the answers often recalled the things you wanted to forget.

The clank of the lift mechanism engaging alerted Mrs Pritchard to her master's imminent return. Her vigil had endured for most of the night and it would soon be sunrise. Uncertain of what to expect when the lift arrived, she raised her gun in readiness and her maids followed suit.

The Doctor was prepared for a reception committee when they resurfaced in the house, but to his surprise he found that he and Ace were taking a back seat. As soon as the hall slid down into view, Josiah, who was still lying in apparent coma, leapt up from the floor. He flung open the

94

gates and wrenched the lift's control lever from its place on the wall.

'I've sealed the lower observatory,' he growled. 'Let Control rot down there!'

As he stumbled forward from the lift, the maids dropped their aim on the Doctor and clustered to support their ailing master.

Mrs Pritchard clutched his trembling hand, sending out a shower of dust. 'You are ill, sir. What must we do?'

'It's getting late,' he croaked. 'Secure the house. I must change!'

Mrs Pritchard indicated the stairs and the maids hurried the invalid away under her guidance. Gwendoline, descending the stairs, met the cortège midway and was ignored for all the pains of her enquiries.

'We won't see them again before nightfall,' muttered the Doctor to Ace. He crouched down beside Nimrod, who still lay unconscious on the lift floor.

'Shouldn't we follow them?' she asked. 'What about Josiah?'

'He sounded a little husky to me.'

Ace was exhausted, but she couldn't help grinning. 'You mean he's changing into one of those things in the cellar.'

The Doctor shrugged. 'I expect he'll shake it off by evening.'

Between them, they began to carry the heavy burden of Nimrod across the hall towards the drawing room. Seeing Gwendoline watching them through the banisters, the Doctor invited her down to join them. She glanced back up the stairs for a second and then descended to follow them into the Josiah's deserted parlour.

They laid Nimrod on the couch and the Doctor busied himself giving the Neanderthal a thorough examination. All that seemed to interest Gwendoline was how soon Nimrod could be woken. She asked the question repeatedly, which irritated Ace so much that she buried her head in the first book she could find. The Reverend Baden-Powell's *Essays on the Unity of Worlds* looked a promising title, but she soon

95

found herself spending longer in the glossary of terms than on the text.

'Don't rush me, Gwendoline,' complained the Doctor as she enquired after Nimrod for the umpteenth time. 'The sun has got its hat on and we have the whole day before Uncle Josiah dares show his face again.'

He was too involved in his examination to notice Gwendoline's nervous reaction. She began to edge her way across the room towards the heavily draped curtain behind the piano.

Ace had at last found something relevant in her book. 'Look, Professor,' she interrupted, pointing to an entry in the glossary, 'Josiah's lucifugous.'

The Doctor smiled indulgently. 'And he doesn't like light either.'

Ace slumped down into an armchair and asked, 'What about the spaceship? It's knackered, isn't it?'

'I just turned off the power,' he confessed. 'Josiah knows about as much of its workings as a hamburger knows about the Amazon desert.'

'Sounds like you and the TARDIS,' she yawned.

Gwendoline had tentatively pushed aside the curtain. Through the bars on the outside of the window, beyond the giant silhouettes of the cedars across the pitch black lawn, she saw the first glimmerings of dawn in the sky.

'Light!' she panicked, fluttering her hands at the glass like the toy bird in her room. She turned and ran from the room.

'Let her go,' said the Doctor, but Ace only grunted and made no attempt to move. 'Come on, Ace, I've only just started,' he said, beginning to pace the room. 'There still one thing you haven't told me. What frightened you so much when you first came to this house in a hundred years' time?'

Feet first! In at the deep end again, he thought guiltily, but the flood of complaints and abuse never came. When he looked, Ace was already fast asleep in her chair.

'Poor Ace,' he said aloud, and he tucked her discarded dinner-jacket around her.

The gaslights throughout the house suddenly guttered and went out. It would soon be day and the Doctor had the run of the house. Either Josiah felt himself secure enough not to care what the Doctor did or he had overlooked the fact in the throes of his latest transformation. The Doctor suspected the former. He had not forgotten that the Reverend Ernest Matthews was no longer in evidence. He doubted that the sanctimonious dean had given Josiah his blessing and departed home for Oxford. More likely, he had already met some untimely fate of his enemy's devising and earned a place in Foxe's *Book of Martyrs*.

Perusing the house, the Doctor paused in the dining room to examine the contents of the cheese dish. He scraped off the film of blue mould that covered the fresh Cheddar and cut himself a slice. He wondered where he should start work: above stairs, below stairs or below the house altogether.

The Reverend Ernest Matthews of Mortarhouse College, Oxford, was slumbering like an ancient child. Seated in the upper observatory, he was oblivious to the dawn light seeping under the window blinds. Nor did he see the pistol that aimed at his head, a gloved finger slowly pressing the trigger. The barrel shifted sideways at the last moment, the gun fired and a bullet passed through the inner circle of a target drawn over a portrait of the Empress of India. The lectern on which the target rested shuddered and a spray of plaster flew from the bullet-riddled wall behind.

Ernest opened his eyes, blinking and unperturbed by his new surroundings.

'So here you are at last,' he observed. 'Haven't I been kept waiting long enough?'

Josiah faced him across a small table. He was smiling faintly and dabbing at his mouth with a handkerchief. His skin was flaky and yellow like old paper, but his eyes, although watering heavily, looked out with the eager intent of a new and vigorous creature beneath the desiccated crust.

Sensing no immediate threat of interruption, Ernest

continued, 'I perceive that you are a sick man, sir. Retribution, no doubt, for your blasphemy.'

'It will pass,' whispered Josiah.

'And so will your unholy theories of evolution. It is a complete absurdity that the line of my ancestors can be traced back to a protoplasmic globule!'

Josiah's smile grew broader. 'Please do go on,' he insisted and slid a silver dish of fruit across the table towards his guest.

'Man has been the same, sir, since he stood in the Garden of Eden . . .' Ernest eyed the fruit and selected a large banana which he proceeded to peel as he lectured, '. . . and he was never, ever a chattering, gibbering ape!'

He impulsively chomped into the banana and then looked up in annoyance. Josiah had begun to wheeze with uncontrollable and triumphant laughter.

'What are you laughing at?' remonstrated the dean, his mouth full. 'The devil take you, why are you laughing!'

Gravely insulted, he glanced down at the hands holding the banana. They were not his hands – they were the wrinkled, black-nailed hands of a monkey all covered in fur.

Josiah's laughter grew louder still as the primate, face aghast, began to dribble fruit down his reverent chin.

Shoes clattered on the wooden stairs and Gwendoline emerged into the observatory. Ernest drew up his legs in fright and squatted on the seat of the chair, resting his knuckles next to his shoes. Unable to believe this nightmare, he stared around and scratched at his sideburns. He was ashamed that he could not resist reaching for another banana.

'Gwendoline,' crooned Josiah, 'come here, my dear child.'

She obeyed and knelt at her guardian's side, so glad to find herself back at the heart of her family. 'Are you unwell, Uncle?' she enquired. Beneath his dried translucent skin, she could just make another form moving, like a snake about to slough its skin.

He stroked her cheek gently, making certain that Ernest could see her response to his affection.

'Only sick at heart, my dear. But soon I shall restore the blighted British Empire to full vigour and glory.' He pointed to the strange apparition that gaped at them from across the table.

'You – you're no better than animals!' protested Ernest with difficulty through his growing teeth. He inadvertently let out a whoop like a startled gibbon and looked away, ashamed and thoroughly miserable.

'The Reverend Ernest Matthews!' proclaimed Josiah. 'I thought he would amuse me. But he makes a tedious toy, don't you think? He bores me just as much as he did before.'

Revelling in anticipation, Gwendoline extracted a dainty handkerchief from her sleeve and folded it into a pad. 'Dear uncle,' she said, and smiled knowingly into his eyes.

'We're so glad he has to go away,' whispered Josiah in her ear. He took a small bottle of brown glass from his pocket and held it aloft.

'And where is he going?' she responded. This was one game she had not forgotten. She watched him uncork the bottle and tip the contents over her handkerchief.

'To Java!' he said.

Ernest Matthews saw Gwendoline, his ministering angel, rise up and move towards him. He stared uncomprehending as she moved in and thrust the pad over his simian face. As darkness overcame him, he heard Josiah eagerly croaking, 'That's the way to the zoo!'

Gabriel Chase was still recumbent in the fleeting shadows of night. From the dark edifice that stood against the roseate sky, only one light shone. It came from behind the blinds that shielded the windows of the upper observatory. Suddenly it too was gone. There was a final distant cry from the Reverend Ernest Matthews and then, moments later, a thrush began its morning song.

* * *

'Miss? Miss?'

Sunlight streamed into Ace's eyes as she woke. She blinked and tried to focus on the figure that was pulling a curtain back from the window.

'Hallo?' she said warily. She then realized that she was lying in bed and wearing a long nightdress.

The figure turned around; Ace saw a chubby woman with friendly rosy cheeks smiling down at her. She wore a mop cap and an apron, but it was not the cold, starched uniform of the maids at Gabriel Chase: hers was cheerful and homely.

Ace thought for a moment that she was out of the dreadful house until she recognized the furniture and doll's house that she remembered from Gwendoline's bedroom. She had not the remotest idea how she had got there and didn't like to ask.

'The Doctor said you'd be fair famished when you woke up,' said the housekeeper, advancing with a tray. 'So here's scrambled eggs, hot buttered toast, kedgeree, kidneys, sausage, bacon, porridge and cream.' She set the loaded tray on the eiderdown in front of Ace and stood back proudly.

'Cholesterol city!' exclaimed Ace, relieved that the food wasn't all on one plate.

The housekeeper frowned. 'Oh no, dear. Perivale village.'

She watched the pretty young lady tuck in enthusiastically and then readjusted a vase of rosebuds she had set on the dressing table.

'Properly exhausted you were when I put you to bed,' she fussed. 'Oh, I nearly forgot. There's a message: would you join the Doctor and the police-gentleman in the drawing room.'

'Police?' said Ace. Surely the Old Bill were the last people the Doctor would bother with – unless someone else had called them.

The housekeeper was nodding with approval. 'It's high time they were called if you ask me. I said as much to my husband, Mr Grose.'

Ace, who wished there was some brown sauce for the bacon, sniffed dismissively. 'I think I might give that one a miss. I want to have a look round Perivale village before lunch. Is there a blacksmith on the green?'

'Mercy no, dearie,' smiled Mrs Grose. 'There's only seven houses and the church! And besides, you've missed lunch. It must be all of five o'clock by now.'

Ace dropped her fork. 'What!' she said.

'Nearly evening,' continued Mrs Grose. 'So we must hurry. No one in their right head stays in this house after dark.'

'Is that what the Doctor's been saying?' snapped Ace.

Mrs Grose pulled the tray clear as the girl leapt out of bed in a panic and started to hunt through the dresses in the wardrobe.

'Where's my clobber?' Ace demanded. The housekeeper looked bewildered. 'My gear . . . clothes!' insisted Ace.

Mrs Grose smiled indulgently. 'Those shabby old things? The Doctor had me lay out this for you.' She produced a long, white, summer dress from the wardrobe: it was elegantly simple with black, embroidered borders on the skirt and bodice. 'Will it do, my dear?' she asked.

Ace fanned out the dress and knew when she was beaten. 'No bustle,' she grinned. 'OK Professor, you win.' She held the dress up to herself in front of the mirror. It was a knockout.

Mrs Grose glowed. 'That's right. Much more fitting for a young lady.'

To Ace's horror, she saw the housekeeper in the mirror advancing on her armed with a whalebone corset.

Beside her, the cut roses had come into full bloom.

The Doctor had been busy. He had set himself an agenda of tasks for the day and had already been well ahead of schedule, when he heard the key in the front door and found Mrs Grose, the day housekeeper, arriving in the hall. He always had time for servants. Always ask the cleaners if you wanted information about a place, that was his motto. Cleaners were the eyes and ears of any community; true to

101

form, Mrs Grose had been a mine of information. She was charmed by the Doctor, whom she felt to be the first real gentleman to enter Gabriel Chase since she couldn't remember when. She had immediately made him tea.

Through her complaints and grumbles, she was soon divulging all manner of secrets about the house: doors that were always locked; the master, Mr Smith, who was an invalid recluse and whom she had never met; guests who arrived, but who she never saw depart, even if they sometimes left their baggage behind. Most of this she did not understand, but she recognized the place's unsavoury nature all right. There were blocks on her mind of course, just like all the other humans in the house; Josiah was not risking interference from a group of local peasants.

Fortunately, Mrs Grose knew her place and refrained from pestering the Doctor with too many questions. He persuaded her to put the exhausted Ace to bed upstairs while he tried to get on with some of his other more pressing tasks.

Of all these, the task he was most to regret was the waking quite so early of Josiah's specimen of a Victorian police inspector. It took about ten minutes to rouse Inspector Alfred Mackenzie of Scotland Yard from the static trance in which he had been preserved, catalogued and consigned to a display drawer.

The Doctor's initial misgivings came when Mackenzie opened his twinkling blue eyes for the first time, smoothed his handle-bar moustache and said, 'And you are . . . ?' The inspector was completely unaware of his fate and was mainly concerned with the unaccountable pangs of hunger with which he was wracked.

It was useless trying to explain recent events in the house to Mackenzie. His straightforward mind needed solid facts, but at Gabriel Chase the solid facts would overwhelm his sanity altogether.

'Typical humans!' muttered the Doctor. 'If they don't understand it, they block it out completely. No wonder Josiah has it so easy.'

He decided there and then not to talk to himself out

loud, because Mackenzie had already produced a notebook and was licking the tip of a pencil.

As far as the inspector was concerned, it was two years ago and he had just arrived at Gabriel Chase to start his investigation. Sir George Pritchard, the owner of the house, had disappeared in curious circumstances and his wife, Lady Margaret, had summoned the police. Mackenzie had been speaking to her, but she had also vanished. The next thing he knew this strange Doctor had appeared from nowhere and taken over the running of the house. Mackenzie began to suspect the foulest of play. There was no body yet, but he was quick to add the Doctor to his list of suspects for that eventuality. Determined to get to the bottom of the mystery before some half-baked private sleuth arrived, he decided to continue his inquiry in the kitchen where, in all likelihood, there might be the chance of a meal.

This allowed the Doctor to complete several tricky tasks that he wanted kept secret for the moment. Even indoors, the warmth and sunshine of a tranquil day in late summer were enough to dull the sinister threat of the house at night. From the second floor of the house, the view across the countryside presented a pastoral paradise. The harvest had been collected weeks ago and despite the heat, the trees were showing the first golden hints of autumn. Beyond the parkland, the fields swept south, down to the River Brent and west across to Horsenden Hill. Perivale, Greenford Parva or Pear Tree Valley, whatever it was called; the Doctor was depressed to imagine how this rural idyll would, within a hundred years, be swamped by the faceless world of housing estates that Ace would be born into.

But the darkness had to be confronted. The Control creature would not stay entombed in the stone spaceship for ever, and the Doctor could guess why the door to the upper observatory was locked. The menace both within and beneath the house had not been stilled; its secrets tantalized the Doctor, just as the whole universe played havoc with his curiosity. He had to know the answers.

Of his set tasks, only one had eluded the Doctor. Nimrod

still lay unconscious on the couch in the drawing room. Thank goodness Mrs Grose had not wanted to clean in there. Between other jobs, the Doctor had made repeated attempts to break the manservant's trance, but to no avail. At about five o'clock, when Mrs Grose had taken a tray of food up to Ace on his instructions, he tried again. Nimrod was still infuriatingly resistant. If the Doctor hadn't known better, he would have said it was deliberate.

He was staring into the depths of Nimrod's inert brown eye, when he heard the drawing room door open and Mackenzie's voice enquire, 'You say this house is owned by Josiah Samuel Smith?'

The Doctor released Nimrod's eyelid and got warily to his feet. 'No, inspector,' he announced with clipped tones, 'I didn't say owned; I said inhabited.'

Mackenzie, still in full dress uniform and cap, waved a half-eaten beef sandwich at the Doctor in frustration. 'Then where is he? The whole house is deserted.' He finished off the sandwich and placed a plate with another three on a side table.

'He will appear,' grunted the Doctor and returned to his patient.

Mackenzie sidled up and eyed Nimrod from a safe distance. 'The manservant, you say. Nasty looking customer. Must be a foreigner.'

'Neanderthal,' observed the Doctor.

Mackenzie nodded. 'Gypsy blood. I can see it in him. They're lazy workers. What's this one playing up about?'

'He's mesmerized.'

'No self control these Mediterraneans: too excitable; nasty tempers too,' confirmed the inspector.

'Only when roused,' snapped the Doctor, struggling to keep his own temper, 'which is exactly what is eluding me at the moment!' So this was the spirit of the British Empire that ruled half the planet. Mackenzie had probably read about foreigners in the *London Illustrated News*.

Mackenzie shrugged and fetched another beef sandwich while the Doctor busied himself testing the manservant's reflexes. The inspector peered in close over his shoulder.

'I'm busy, inspector,' complained the Doctor.

'And I have my investigation to complete.'

Once again the Doctor rose. With a fixed smile he asked, 'Still not found the mustard then?' Mackenzie looked blankly back, so he continued. 'Since I woke you up, you have consumed three full English breakfasts and a four-course lunch. If you're still hungry, get Mrs Grose to make us some afternoon tea.'

The inspector finished off the sandwich and produced his notebook from a pocket. 'She's hiding facts from me,' he asserted. 'And so are you. If you don't tell me where the rest of the household are, I'll arrest you for obstructing my inquiries!'

Ace could hear the argument as she came down the stairs. She was still trying to adjust to walking in the dress and corset; there must be a knack to it, she thought, if only she could work it out. Deportment, however, had never been on the curriculum at school.

As she reached the hall, she also thought she heard a scrabbling noise coming from the direction of the lift. But the rumpus from the drawing room was enough to drown anything else. Besides which, Ace was not happy about missing out on what the Doctor was doing. After being tricked back to Gabriel Chase, she was not sure she wanted to let him out of her sight.

She opened the drawing room door and saw the Doctor coming towards her. Ace thought he faltered for a second as if he had expected someone but not necessarily her. Nimrod was still flat out on the sofa and a shortish man in old-fashioned police uniform was standing beside him, watching her.

'Professor, you could have woken me sooner,' she said.

The Doctor gently took her arm and confided, 'This is Inspector Mackenzie of Scotland Yard. He was summoned here in 1881 to investigate the disappearance of the owner, Sir George Pritchard.'

Ace was incredulous. 'But that's two years ago!' she protested.

'He was in one of Josiah's cabinets,' whispered the Doctor. 'Preserved; hypnotized: humour him.' He raised his eyes to heaven and left her to cope.

A preserved policeman! Life was never easy with the Doctor. She looked across at the inspector. 'Hallo,' she said. 'All right?'

'Inspector, this is my friend Ace,' intervened the Doctor. 'I like the dress,' he added to her. 'How did you sleep?'

Mackenzie approached, notebook at the ready. Ace saw the Doctor moving towards Nimrod for safety.

'Perhaps you can tell me where Lady Pritchard is, miss.'

Ace looked at the Doctor. 'Does he mean that old bag the housekeeper?' she asked. The Doctor waved his hands, indicating that she should talk to the inspector.

'I gather you live in Perivale village,' continued Mackenzie.

Police inquiries into her private life brought back too many awkward memories for Ace.

'I'll be moving to the area . . . sometime,' she answered coldly. She moved over to join the Doctor. 'How's Tarzan?' she asked, looking at Nimrod.

'No change,' he muttered. 'He's still out like a light.' Nimrod's eyelids flickered for a second.

The Doctor leaned in close to the Neanderthal's hairy ear. 'Light,' he said.

Nimrod's hand shot out and grasped Ace's arm like a vice. She cried out and tried to pull away, but she was held tight.

'Don't move!' hissed the Doctor.

Ace looked at Nimrod and found herself staring directly into the brown pools of his eyes.

It was clear that the last thing Nimrod could see was Ace. He gasped, half choked and seemed to stare straight through her. Then with a deep breath, he began to speak in the deep rich tones of a voice that was years, centuries, even millennia away.

'I am the memory teller of our tribe. I keep the embers of each story in my mind, so that they burn fresh with each telling.'

'Good Lord,' exclaimed the astonished inspector.

Ace was too frightened to move.

The Doctor hurriedly began to rummage through Nimrod's jacket pockets. 'Word association,' he muttered. 'Somehow I've triggered him off.' Finally, he produced the ancient, yellow bear's tooth from the waistcoat. Placing the ritual symbol in Nimrod's other hand, he said, 'Nimrod, the fang of the cave bear calls you. Tell us your tale.'

Mackenzie hurriedly turned to a new page in his notebook.

Nimrod's attention focused on the tooth, relaxing his grip on Ace's arm enough for her to pull away. So intrigued were all three spectators, that they failed to notice a shadow pressing against the gap between the doors to the hall. It breathed quickly but silently as it recovered from the exertion of its long climb.

Nimrod swung his legs down from the couch and sat clasping the tooth in both hands, staring as he saw it flickering in the precious firelight of his native time. There were his long-lost, brown-eyed people; spears waved in greeting as they issued from the cave village to meet him. The sunlight was pale through the forest trees; cold under the ominous gathering of snow clouds. The people sat silently waiting for the memory teller to begin. Most of his tales were old, passed down the generations, word for word, but today this was his own tale and he was the first to tell it.

'At the season when the ice floods swamped the pasture lands, we herded the mammoths sunwards to find new grazing.'

'Tricky things, mammoths,' endorsed Mackenzie.

'As the snows hid the green world, the eating grew lean. The wise men cast bones to make hunting magic and spoke with the voice of the Burning One.'

Ace struggled to find a rational explanation for Nimrod's behaviour. 'Is this a race memory?' she whispered to the Doctor.

He emphatically shook his head. 'No, these are his real experiences.'

Nimrod's mind clouded. His family, his people and his world were long dead. They lived only in his thoughts now. If he lost their memory, they were gone for ever. He was alone; and after him . . . Clinging in vain to the tooth, his thoughts turned to despair.

'But now the wild world is lost in a desert of smoke and straight lines. There is smoke sickness, but Light will return.'

'Light will return.'

Only the Doctor heard the growled echo from outside the drawing room doors.

Nimrod fell silent; he slid sideways to rest his head which teemed with memories on the stack of cushions.

Much relieved, the inspector stretched and rubbed the back of his neck; he felt peckish.

As soon a she had heard the word light, Ace felt a chill of fear in her stomach. She had hoped after waking to find all the hate and evil swept away from the house, but it was all starting again. By now the Doctor would be in it up to his neck. All she wanted was to get out before something else happened.

There was a scream from the hall.

9

Out of Control

Mrs Grose came down the stairs with a vase of withered roses, tutting at the trail of fallen petals she left behind her. Halfway down she froze; there was a shape, a tall mound of greying rags, pressed against the drawing room doors. As she stepped closer, Mrs Grose heard soft growling noises and a low whine.

'Who are you!' she challenged.

The shape turned and hissed. Mrs Grose saw a snarling face, half covered by rags, but grey and mottled like the moon. It rushed towards her and she screamed.

The Doctor dashed out of the drawing room to find Mrs Grose, hand to mouth, standing amid the dead roses. Across the hall, the lift gates were closing.

'Oh, sir,' she gasped as he and Ace helped her to a chair. 'Oh Lord, I've never seen the like.'

'Brandy,' snapped the Doctor to Mackenzie.

The inspector produced a hip-flask from his jacket and handed it over.

'What did you see, ma'am?' he asked.

Mrs Grose watched the Doctor pour a large tot into the cupped top and moaned, 'Oh, it was a horrible thing – horrible.' She took the cup and sipped at the brandy amid reassurances from the Doctor. Then a doleful expression came over her face. 'Have I been wicked, sir?' she asked.

'Of course not,' said the Doctor patiently. 'Just try to tell us what happened.'

Mrs Grose forced herself to finish the brandy and then said, 'It was waiting there by the door, all hunched up and horrible. And then it hissed and spat like a hellcat. It was a wicked, wicked thing!'

'Control,' guessed Ace. 'But how did it get up here?'

'Like the very devil itself it was, miss,' added Mrs Grose, holding out the cup to the Doctor in hope of a recharge.

'You like a little drop, do you Mrs Grose?' asked the inspector.

'I beg your pardon, sir.'

Entirely missing the proffered cup, the Doctor intervened. 'Inspector, Mrs Grose is a god-fearing woman. I'm sure she has told us everything she saw.'

'Thank you, Doctor,' said the housekeeper. She rose from the chair and smoothed out her apron. 'I shan't be staying a moment longer. I must seek employment elsewhere.'

'Very wise,' agreed the Doctor. 'And when you do, give my regards to Peter Quint . . .'

She gave him a curious look, bobbed to both him and Ace and disappeared towards the kitchen to collect her things.

The Doctor smiled: the staff were deserting the house. That was another turn of the screw in Josiah's coffin.

'Professor!' whispered Ace urgently and pointed to the lift. The Doctor, however, shushed her to be quiet.

Mackenzie pocketed his flask and announced, 'This madhouse needs one more good going over.'

'Good idea,' agreed the Doctor, shepherding him towards the stairs. 'Try to be back by six o'clock.'

'Why's that?'

'Because round here, the forces of darkness don't wait until midnight to appear!'

Completely flummoxed, Mackenzie ascended the stairs and disappeared.

With relief, the Doctor turned to Ace.

'I know, I know!' he asserted before she could start. He could see that a grey shape was still lurking inside the

110

closed lift. They could hear it breathing. The Doctor raised his voice especially for its benefit.

'Climbing up the lift shaft's very clever! I'd hoped the Control creature might bring something with it. But for that it'll need the lift!'

There was a pause and then the clank of machinery as the lift suddenly began to descend.

Ace couldn't understand. 'I thought the lift was broken,' she said.

'I mended it.' He walked back across the hall into the drawing room with Ace in pursuit.

'Professor! What's going on?' She almost felt like crying she was so confused.

He flapped his hands to quieten her while he thought out loud. 'Josiah and Control are afraid of it. Redvers Fenn-Cooper saw it and lost his reason. Nimrod worships it.'

'Let there be Light?' asked Ace.

'It's asleep down there in its spaceship and Josiah doesn't want it woken.'

'Well, maybe that's a good idea. Maybe it should be left alone, Professor – just this once.'

'It must be very, very old,' he mused. 'Perhaps even older.' He looked at her with imploring eyes. 'Just a little chat . . .'

'Professor!' she protested, but she knew it was a lost battle. She sat on the couch and then noticed that Nimrod had vanished. 'Where's Tarzan?' she asked.

The Doctor sniffed. 'Gone to see a man about a god,' he said sulkily.

Something chirruped. Both the Doctor and Ace suddenly became conscious of a high stridulant sound that was coming from one of the display cabinets. Before Ace could stop him, the Doctor had pulled open a drawer.

Ace jumped back in disgust as the wing of a large moth brushed her face. The drawer was crawling with insects which were no longer in their regimented, preserved ranks, but very much alive. Several emerald-winged butterflies fluttered past her; crickets sprang from their prison; huge Amazonian cockroaches and a repulsive millipede were scrambling over the edge, antennae waving. Ace was revolted.

'It's the energy from the spaceship, isn't it?' she guessed. 'It's bringing it all alive!'

'Go and find Mackenzie,' ordered the Doctor. 'Things are hotting up sooner than I anticipated.'

Journal Entry. September 20th, 1883.

. . . precious little has gone right with me since I left England. No sign of Redvers, nor will there ever be now, but I glimpsed the Doctor earlier and greeted him as best I could in my doleful state. He called me Redvers and says I am naturally of a melancholy disposition. I beseeched him to join my expedition, but he declined, preferring to travel alone.

The moon is setting over the veldt. In these parts, night is often as bright as day. Earlier, a scorpion crawled out from behind the brass bedrail. It scuttled towards me, but I crushed it with Redvers' boot. The forest is alive with noise tonight. The chorus of cicadas is enough to drive any man to madness.

To my astonishment, a native in full dinner-jacket has emerged from a door in the undergrowth. Am I then to perish on the spear of this barbarous savage? He falters. By heaven, I believe that salvation is at hand!

Nimrod saw Redvers Fenn-Cooper watching the sunset from the window. He was seated on the bare floor, still bound in the strait-jacket. On seeing the manservant, he looked startled for a moment and then cried, 'Redvers knew the relief column would arrive!'

Nimrod reverently bowed to the mad explorer. A great fear had come upon him since he had seen his people once again. Their stern eyes had warned him: you carry our memories, we must not be lost. Bewildered, he knew he must seek advice, but his new ways, the ways of the servant, were not easily cast aside.

112

'Excuse me, sir,' he asked, 'you speak with the wildness of the old world. Is it appropriate to seek your wisdom?'

'You won't get far without good supplies,' began Redvers. 'Baggage animals, porters . . .'

'The one I serve sir, the Burning One, is waking. What should I do?'

Redvers knew the answer immediately. 'Stanley found Livingstone. I found Redvers . . . once. You must hunt the dark continent, seek out what you desire. But be warned . . . you may find it!'

From his jacket, Nimrod produced a large hunting knife. Redvers pulled back, fearing betrayal. 'I must free you from your bonds, sir,' insisted the manservant.

Redvers flung his jacketed arms wide. 'The Doctor did that hours ago!' he laughed. 'Redvers only wears this against the cold of the night air.'

There was a click behind them. The handle on the door in the undergrowth turned back and forth.

Inspector Mackenzie cursed; every room in this wretched house was sealed up. He left the door and stamped further along the passage. The air was humid and he felt as if he was suffering from prickly heat. He climbed to the second floor but it was just as deserted. It seemed to have been a long day, but he must find Lady Margaret again before he went to fetch reinforcements from Scotland Yard.

He was trying another door when a nightbird shrieked and heavy wings beat over his head. He ducked and saw that there was nothing to avoid. He was getting jumpy; the unceasing gaze of the stuffed birds that filled the place made him very uneasy.

'Inspector,' called Ace, and he jumped. 'Found anything?' she asked, rounding the corner.

Mackenzie clutched his heart and longed for something simple, like a reassuring brawl in a chop-house.

'Nothing,' he said. 'This house has more locked doors than Reading jail.'

Immediately, the door he had just tried opened slowly of its own volition to reveal a flight of stairs leading upwards.

'It's to the upper observatory,' said Ace and led the way. Mackenzie followed her. Once he was through the door closed silently after them.

The Doctor sensed the welling of energy beneath the house, like a dam about to burst. He had set the wheels in motion and was reduced to waiting for the outcome. It had been a busy day, but as long as he could trust Control, and as long as it – or rather she – trusted him, then it might yet prove worthwhile. He said she, because he was sure that was what the unfortunate creature was becoming. She had snarled and hissed through the locked gates of the mended lift when he had visited the basement earlier for one of his little chats. But she must find her own way to complete their bargain if she wanted what he had offered; he would not help. Ace would be furious of course, but he had to know what was sleeping in the spaceship, and there seemed no better way of stopping Josiah's meddling.

He passed the time in the study consoling one of the South American cockroaches; he assured it that all civilisation started with hunting and foraging. Everything had a chance to work its way up.

That'll be the phone, he thought. He put the insect down and after a moment the device rang.

'No, I haven't forgotten our agreement,' he told the caller. 'I'm ready when you are.' He was alerted by a sudden click and said, 'Wait. There's someone else on the line.' But Control had gone. The line clicked once more and the Doctor knew that his bargain had been overheard. Again he felt the surge of energy as it moved through the fabric of the house. It was too late to stop now.

The glowing miasma in the lower observatory swirled with gold and the crystal outcrops pulsed with energy. The ship groaned its birth pangs as the blinding effulgence centred on the membrane core; the shadow inside convulsed in furious spasms. Before it, crouched over the crystal console, was Control, angrily summoning the husks to her side and her support.

'Move! Move! Time moving faster than you!'

114

The great brutes lumbered up, rocking from one foot to the other like a monstrous guard of honour.

'Light angry, burning angry! But not with poor Control!'

Her gloved claws moved with certainty over the crystals. She was afraid, but the Doctor had promised and she would bind him to his word. She was changing too. No longer trapped, she had a new purpose.

'Control going showing light way up. Then Control on way up too!'

The crystals were moving by themselves now. The ship roared in pain, spurting steam. Control screamed and the membrane split across, flooding the ship with the blazing rage of Light.

The hand that snapped the telephone receiver back onto its stand was fleshy pink and well manicured. The third finger wore a signet ring bearing the entwined initials G and M. It tapped the stand in contemplation and then withdrew as the stairs clattered with ascending feet.

Ace hardly recognized the upper observatory as she led the inspector up into the high, domed chamber. The TARDIS still stood to the side, but other items of furniture had been covered by dust sheets, as if the owner was planning to spend winter away.

'No one up here either,' observed Mackenzie, but Ace was not convinced. She tugged away a sheet, unleashing a cloud of dust. A grey, translucent shape lay in a chair, inert in its filthy velvet jacket.

'Disgusting object,' said Mackenzie. 'What is it?'

The object's features were all too familiar to Ace; she began to feel ill.

'It's what's left of Josiah Smith. It's just a husk.' She knew the significance of the cast skin and began warily to look round.

'I think we should get out of here,' she said quietly.

'Nonsense young lady, that thing's not dangerous,' blustered Mackenzie and he pulled away another dust sheet. Mrs Pritchard, the night housekeeper, sat there immobile in gaunt black, her eyes lifeless and staring.

'Lady Margaret!' he exclaimed.

'Lady!' echoed Ace.

'Sir George Pritchard's wife,' he confirmed. But the figure looked so gaunt and tired; hardly the proud and handsome woman he had spoken with that morning. Only that morning was like a distant memory.

Ace angrily snatched away the final sheet to reveal the pale little figure kneeling on the floor beside the housekeeper.

'Gwendoline. She's their daughter, isn't she?'

'What's happening in this house?' demanded Mackenzie. Suddenly he had three dead bodies and was thrice as confused.

Ace wanted to touch Gwendoline's cold face, but could not bring herself near it. 'They're just his toys! Josiah's toys!' she choked and crossed the room away from the horrific tableau.

Set aside from the three figures there was a large rectangular shape draped in another sheet. Ace read the brass plaque at its base: *Homo Victorianus Ineptus*, and turned back; she did not want to see.

Mackenzie, who had followed her, pulled back the cloth. In a glass case, crouching in dried grass with one hairy hand resting on a branch and the other holding a half-peeled banana, was the Reverend Ernest Matthews. Champion of mankind's supremacy over nature, enemy of Darwinism, he was devolved in cruel mockery of his belief. His preserved body was displayed as a startled, sad-eyed ape.

Mackenzie backed away; Ace thought she would throw up.

Instead, they heard the distant chimes of the clock. Mackenzie looked at his watch, which had stopped; surely, however, it was not already six o'clock.

From their places, Gwendoline and Mrs Pritchard were rising like predators.

'Get out!' yelled Ace, but Gwendoline caught her by the arm and they fought like wildcats.

'Let go of her, madam!' shouted Mackenzie, producing a gun, but Mrs Pritchard's arm scythed out and sent him

116

tumbling back against the seated husk. Its leathery arms, still full of vigour, clamped around him and he lost his weapon.

Undeterred, he yelled, 'I am a police officer! You will do what I tell you! Reinforcements are on the way!'

Ace had managed to push Gwendoline away against her mother, but as she turned to run, she saw a new horror emerging from the TARDIS. It was Josiah Samuel Smith; his face was fresh and ruddy, his hair a lush auburn colour and his clothes immaculate. He smirked and his eyes twinkled evilly.

Ace dashed in a frenzy for the window. 'Stitch this, Dracula!' she shouted and released the blind. It snapped up, catching the monster in the last rays of the setting sun.

He flung his arms wide in triumph. 'I no longer need to crouch in the shadows, young lady!' he crowed.

In despair Ace ran at him, but Mrs Pritchard caught her hair and dragged her back. Ace slashed at Josiah's face with her fingers, but was held fast.

'You're no gentleman,' she told him. 'Scratch the Victorian veneer and something nasty'll come crawling out!'

He grabbed her by the chin, forcing her to look him in the eye. She could still hear the distant clock chiming far beyond its allotted span.

'Your beloved Doctor thinks to get the better of me,' he hissed. 'But I'll see him squirming yet! Bring her!' he ordered Mrs Pritchard.

He headed away down the stairs followed by his housekeeper, his ward and their prisoner. Trapped in the chair, the inspector struggled to escape.

Sensing the emergent focus of energy beneath the house, the Doctor knew he could wait no longer. He had hoped to find Ace in the hall, but instead he saw Nimrod waiting by the lift gates. The Neanderthal had not seen Ace and seemed unconcerned; he had determined to seek the truth from the Burning One. Nimrod's personal enlightenment was not top of the Doctor's list at that moment, but he advised the manservant to stick around; it would save him a trip.

'Can you summon it then?' Nimrod asked, still incredulous that so strange a figure could wield such power.

The Doctor winked. 'Let's just say I've made a deal with its agent.'

From the depths came the ominous clank of the lift machinery; the wheels began to grind.

'That should be them now,' added the Doctor. 'Where's Ace got to?'

There was no time to lose, so he had to lose some. The Doctor opened the glass cover of the grandfather clock and pushed the hands forward fifteen minutes to six o'clock.

'It's not dark yet, but I don't want Josiah to miss the show.'

As the clock started to chime, the panels in the walls across the hall opened and the maids issued forth, swishing into their places on the stairs.

The lift cable twitched as the carriage rose nearer, but the clock, having completed six strokes, continued its chimes, soon passing twelve and content, it seemed to strike infinity. The maids sourly regarded the Doctor from their ranks.

Tiring of the chimes, the Doctor reached into the clock and stopped the pendulum. Nimrod stared in awe. 'Doctor, you are as powerful as you are wise,' he said.

'Cut the homespun twaddle, Nimrod,' was the reply. 'This isn't wise. I just lit the blue touch paper and found there's nowhere to retire to.' He turned and bowed to the scowling maids. 'Good evening, ladies. I hope you like indoor fireworks.'

Above the stairs, the stained glass window began to hum and flicker.

'The Burning One is coming!' cried Nimrod.

'Then I should keep well clear of the lift,' advised the Doctor. 'To catch a wolf, I may have unleashed a tiger!'

There was a scuffle on the landing above and Josiah appeared with Gwendoline and Mrs Pritchard who clutched the struggling Ace between them.

118

'Doctor! What are you doing? Stop the lift!' yelled Josiah.

'Josiah Samuel Smith! So you finally evolved into a Victorian. How quaint.' The Doctor was delighted and relieved to have an audience at last, no matter what shape it turned up in. 'And Ace, you got here in time.'

'Sorry, Professor,' she called.

'Don't apologize. Come down and meet Josiah's new guests.'

'Nimrod!' Josiah was pushing down through the advancing maids. 'Stop the lift! Stop it!'

'Much too late for that,' smirked the Doctor. 'It's time to shed a little Light on your plans.'

'No!' Josiah yelled in the Doctor's face. The clanking of the lift stopped and the Doctor turned to walk to the closed gates.

'Hold him!' called Mrs Pritchard. Immediately, two maids seized the Doctor's arms and held him back.

'You've made a pact with that creature!' accused Josiah. 'You don't know what you're doing!'

'But I'll soon find out.' The Doctor looked towards the darkened lift and called, 'You can come out now. We're all waiting.'

The gates swung open and the ragged, grey apparition that was called Control stepped from the dark interior. From under the veils, the half-moon face and animal eye regarded the onlookers and fixed upon Josiah, its hated enemy and opposite.

'Control!' whispered Josiah with utmost malice. 'Quintessence of wickedness. Corruption incarnate!' The two faced each other in mutual loathing.

'Thank you for trusting me, Control,' interrupted the Doctor.

Control drew back her veils to reveal her grey half-formed face. She pulled and twisted the material in her gloved hands in pride at what a clever Control she had been.

'My half greeingment done,' she revelled in her gravelled voice and pointed to the lift. Its doors had closed again. 'You desiring. In the darkness, you find it.'

'Don't let it out!' Josiah launched himself at the gates, but a blast of energy coursed through his very bones and tossed him aside.

'Too late!' gloried Control.

The gates flew open; a core of engulfing brilliance such as even the Doctor had never seen burst upon them.

The humans and would-be-humans screamed and shielded their eyes. Only the Doctor stared direct into the fierce, incandescent heart of Light.

10
Twice upon a Time

Wave upon wave of cold radiance flowed from the fierce
crucible of white in the lift. Fizzing and hissing, the almost
solid brilliance paled, became opaque and finally translucent. A giant figure was discernible in the icy furnace.
Around it glowed an aura of gold, either created by or itself
creating the figure at its heart – the Doctor could not tell
which.

Robed in liquid gold and silver, with skin shimmering, it
had the noble and terrible beauty of a seraph, fallen to
Earth from its place beside the Throne. It glided from the
lift, energy humming from it like a generator and droning
fiercely at any mortal it passed.

Control and Ace shied clear of the luminous presence;
even the Doctor, extending a hand in greeting, fell back
with a cry as the figure passed straight through him.

'Light!' gasped Josiah, scrambling away across the floor
and up the stairs to where his brood of family and staff
watched. Half way up he passed Mackenzie, who had
escaped the clutches of the upper observatory and was on
his awe-struck way down.

Light had reached the far boundary of the hall. It turned
back to observe the onlookers. Within the aura, they saw
its eyes darting and the fingers on its raised hands flexing as
it unceasingly absorbed information. A golden haze diffused
from the aura and drifted past them. It filled the hall with
its glow.

'What the devil is that thing?' whispered Mackenzie to Ace.

'It's an angel, stupid!'

'That's just its shape on Earth,' corrected the Doctor, his eyes fixed on the emanation. 'It's called Light and it's come to survey life here.'

'It was crashed out in its stone spaceship in the basement,' said Ace.

The Doctor nodded. 'But while it slept, the survey got out of control.'

'Control is me!' growled the grey mound of rags at Mackenzie's shoulder.

'And Josiah's the survey,' concluded the Doctor, nodding up the stairs towards the villain.

Determined to have the last word, Ace added, 'Now Light's got to sort out the muddle.'

'That was my idea,' the Doctor boasted.

Mackenzie was perplexed. 'Then who are you?' he demanded.

With a smile, the Doctor replied, 'We wouldn't want to confuse you.'

He stopped short as Control tugged at his sleeve. 'Remember our greeingment. You promise Control's freeness.'

A voice cut through the humming air, high and ethereal, but silky and deadly too. 'Control!' Light had spoken; Control cringed.

'Now! Tell it now!' she insisted.

Once again, Ace began to fear the Doctor. He had made some sort of deal to get this alien Light creature up into the house and she had missed out on it. If she had been there, she would have stopped him. Sometimes he scared the hell out of her.

Light's voice sounded again. 'How long have I been asleep?' It extended a hand towards Control and registered the new shape of its own focal body for the first time. It was astonished. 'Why have I naturalized in this form?'

It was suddenly aware of a threat close by. On the stairs, one of the maids was approaching at Josiah's bidding, her

122

pistol aimed steadily at Light's head. The notion that such a primitive device could harm Light was absurd, but the intention was more dangerous, if only for the assailant. What was Josiah playing at?

The Doctor saw that the maid would be brushed callously aside like a summer fly and yelled, 'No, Light! Don't do it!'

Just a glance was all that was required. The maid's eyes met Light's scrutiny; all colour drained from her and she fell back dead on the stairs. The other maids raised their guns and fired down at the angel, but the weapons clicked uselessly.

'You needn't have done that!' shouted the Doctor.

'Wasteful,' reproved Light. 'Your weapons no longer work.'

'Call them off, Josiah. Come down here and talk,' suggested the Doctor, but Josiah would have none of it.

Urging his servants upward, he led the withdrawal and vanished into the house's warren of passages.

Seeing Light distracted, Mackenzie made a dash for the door. Even before he reached it, however, the bolts snapped home and shutters slammed across the windows. Mackenzie tugged at the handle in vain and turned to see Light staring down at him.

'Nothing leaves until I have explanations,' it said.

As Mackenzie edged back to the rest of the group, the Doctor stepped forward. 'Surely you're not going to tackle that thing?' the inspector muttered.

'I just want a little chat, that's all.'

Light had returned its scrutiny to Control, who sidled forward like a submissive cur. It was apparent that away from Light's influence, Control had been exposed to stimuli that only the Survey Agent was allowed. The proto-creature had grasped the language of this world and begun to resemble the dominant lifestock, but that could be dealt with later.

'This is not the planet I expected,' asserted Light.

'Excuse me, but this is Earth,' interrupted the Doctor.

Light ignored him. 'Our next survey was to be a simple,

123

barren rock with a few social moss colonies and four sterile moons. Easy to catalogue. So why this?'

As Control began to whine, the Doctor heard a voice in his ear. 'You've had your little chat. Let's get out of here.' He pushed Ace away and prayed she would wait a little longer.

It occurred to Ace that she was not the only one who was subjected to initiative tests. By now, Control was going through contortions of misery. 'Poor Control. Always blamed. No hoping.'

'Where is the Survey Agent?' demanded Light. 'What happened while I was dormant?'

'You're still only half awake, Light,' chimed in the Doctor. 'You throw your weight around and you don't even know what planet you're on!'

'What is this?' Light asked, regarding the intruder with curiosity. It was amazed to see the creature disappear out of its view through an entrance portal, pursued by a second of the species dressed in white.

With Ace in tow, the Doctor marched into the drawing room. Assuming that Light was following, he said, 'This is Earth. How many more times! Check the instruments in your ship.' He looked back past Ace and saw that they were not accompanied. 'Now where's he gone?' he complained.

He turned again and started in surprise; Light was ahead of them, its aura pulsing as it waited beside the piano.

'How does Light move so fast?' asked Ace.

The Doctor settled back into a chair. 'He can travel at the speed of . . . thought.'

'Earth!' Light's voice was suddenly steeped in weariness. 'Why mention that wretched planet to me?'

'If you don't like it, then bog off!' Ace met Light's cold stare and tried to back away, but the glare stretched like an arm towards her and she felt as if every muscle and sinew in her body was crushing outwards from within.

'I once spent centuries there faithfully cataloguing every species. Every organism from the smallest bacteria to the largest ichthyosaur. But no sooner had I finished than it was all changing. Growing, crawling and spawning new subspecies – new species! Evolution ran amok! I had to start amending my entries. The task was endless!'

The Doctor shrugged. 'That's life.'

The bright mantle of Light's aura droned louder and the voice deepened with anger. 'Control!'

Thunder rumbled distantly.

The doors flew open on the hall, catching Control, who was spying at the keyhole. She looked up startled and began to whine. Behind her, Mackenzie, whose head was spinning with ideas he could not begin to absorb into a routine enquiry, panicked and fled.

Unable to resist the summons, Control slunk into the room. Light fixed her with its cruel eyes.

'How many more millennia must I endure your company? Is this the Earth?' Control swayed back and forth wringing her gloved hands. 'Well? Where's your other half? Where's the Survey Agent?'

Desperation finally drove Control to protest. 'Control wants freeness! Be a ladylike!' She pointed at the Doctor. 'Doctor promised!'

'It is not his to give.'

Ace knew it; he just couldn't resist, could he? 'Did you promise, Professor?'

The Doctor looked acutely uncomfortable. 'Things ran away with themselves,' he blustered.

'Control too! Run away!' With a final glare at her betrayers, the creature fled into the hall and away up the stairs. Light's head rose to blast its errant charge, but found the Doctor blocking the path.

'Light. Light! Give her a break! She's not the real troublemaker here!' He reached for the angel's arm, but found only insubstantial energy tingling in its form.

'You are interfering,' it growled.

The Doctor was seized by a force that made his body ache. He fought to resist the searing penetration of Light's cold eyes.

'Interfering, just like you,' he said. 'Only I didn't get caught napping!' He tried to stop himself from shaking,

125

but could not look away. 'Forget your survey, Light. Just go!'

The Doctor and Ace were suddenly alone in the silent room. She took his arm for reassurance and said, 'Has he really gone?'

Released from Light's attentions, the Doctor took a deep breath, scowled and said, 'No.'

The house was full of its energy. When he planned to release Light, he should have known it would be a creature cold in heart and mind. It might deal with its renegade experiment, but probably cause untold damage in the process. All things responded to the right influences; he thought of Ace and congratulated himself on how well she was turning out. Control, however she evolved, must be found before either Light or Josiah crushed all the raw potential she embodied.

The rocking horse creaked as Gwendoline swayed to and fro in its saddle, but it was Mrs Pritchard who stood mechanically pulling the toy back and forth by its mane. Josiah had rallied his troops in the upper observatory while he desperately searched for a solution with which to procure his freedom.

'The Doctor is no more human than Light is,' he ranted. 'He's not even British! I wonder which of them is lower in cunning.'

For all the reaction he got, he might as well have talked to the toys. He snapped his fingers in Mrs Pritchard's sullen face.

'But they can both be lured into traps,' she responded.

'Preferably together. The collection is short of predators.'

Staring ahead as she swayed on the horse, Gwendoline said, 'Let me deal with them, uncle. I like traps.'

As footsteps sounded on the stairs, Mrs Pritchard added, 'And Nimrod must be punished for his disobedience.'

'I am here, sir.' The manservant shepherded the bewildered Redvers Fenn-Cooper up into the chamber.

'So you came sneaking back looking for favours,' commented the housekeeper.

Nimrod addressed only his master. 'I know where my allegiance lies, sir.'

'Redvers is here on my instruction, madam,' reprimanded Josiah. He directed Redvers towards the bullet splintered lectern; the explorer smiled in recognition, nodded and gazed at the target that had been set up there. Josiah chuckled. Nothing would stop his plan for the Empire. With luck Light and the Doctor would be at each others' throats before they even noticed.

'Mrs Pritchard will organize dinner and deal with that interfering policeman.'

'Very good, sir.'

'Gwendoline.' He slipped his hands around her waist and lifted her gently down from the horse. 'Time for Miss Ace to leave us.'

Looking up into his eyes, the girl replied, 'I'm sure she'll enjoy Java, Uncle, once she gets there.'

'Not as much as you'll enjoy sending her, my dear.' He turned to the explorer, still engrossed in the target. 'And Redvers Fenn-Cooper?'

'Redvers kicked over his traces and lost himself in the bush. Lord knows if he'll ever find his way out.'

'And your other quest, Redvers?'

Redvers began to stutter in confusion. 'I don't recall . . . the heat haze . . . is dazzling.'

'I need you, Redvers. Stay out of trouble. We've a royal appointment to keep.'

An Asian Atlas moth, attracted by the light, flapped gracefully into the gas flame and burned to death. Redvers returned to his feverish contemplation of the target; behind him, Josiah was wracked with silent laughter.

Beyond the confines of Gabriel Chase, where time had not frozen with a jolt at a minute past six o'clock, the last streaks of day had fled before the relentless march of night. In the house, the stylized green foliage on the drapes and wallpaper of the upstairs passages, glowed in the soft gaslight. Cicadas cree-creeked their night song.

Control sat in an alcove surrounded by stuffed finches

and tanagers which spread their gaudy wings and flew nowhere. She peeled back the greasy rags that covered her face and scratched at her skin; it felt strange, all pins and needles. It was softer as well. But she did not care.

'Poor Control wanted freeness. They promised freeness, but no one gave it. So Control took freeness all on lone! Hers now. No taking it way gain.'

She had soon learned to deal with doors without the help of a husk. By pressing on the handle and pushing, or by simply kicking them in, she was slowly uncovering the secrets of the new world she had escaped into. There was so much to watch, touch, smell, taste and hear; some of it familiar from the pictures and few words she had recognized in *The Times*. 'I have brought you your copy of *The Times*,' or 'Here is your *Times*,' said her grim jailer every day, and although the other patterns changed, the symbol at the top was always the same: *The Times*. Her first words.

Other things in this green world were new: the brightly coloured insects that flew and crawled among the furniture; the high, draped openings that looked onto darkness. Perhaps there was a new world beyond each door. Thrilled, she greedily absorbed all information and put it to good use. Squinting cross-eyed down her snout, she saw that her skin was turning pale and pink. Her nose was less squat and was no longer cold and wet to touch.

Smelling danger, she dodged through a door to avoid the crocodile of maids that passed along the corridor. At their head, Mrs Pritchard paused for a second to listen to the chorus of insects alive in the panelling. Then she led her minions on, down the back stairs to their duties.

Control emerged from hiding and gazed at the wonders of her new world. Crickets hopped from drape to drape; a millipede wound its way along a gilt picture frame; a glossy beetle scuttled across a veneered mahogany table. Control caught the beetle in her glove, popped it into her mouth and crunched happily. It tasted far better than the cockroaches in her cell.

She froze, suddenly aware of a figure pushing towards her through the fronds of a large potted palm. It moved cautiously and held out a handful of sparkling objects in her direction.

'Take them,' said Redvers, offering out the handful of beaded necklaces and bracelets he had found in one of the bedrooms.

Control stared warily at the beads and snatched them away.

'You like them. You keep them,' said Redvers. 'Then we trade words.'

Control looked into Redvers' face, but had no words to say that she might trust him. She held the beads tight in her hands and remembered what they might mean. 'Lady-like?' she said hopefully.

He nodded.

As he led her away from the beaten tracks, hunter leading the hunted, the Doctor and Ace rounded the far corner of the passage. Given half a chance Ace would have legged it by now, but there was no way she was letting the Doctor out of her sight. Of course she was jumpy with so many loonies about: what did he expect? It reminded her more and more of what the house had been like the first time she got in. Up here, the humid air was getting too clammy to breath easily; it had the rich smell of damp earth in a hothouse and the insects were really giving it some stick. It felt alive. It was like the reptile house at the zoo.

The altering state of the house reminded the Doctor of the oppressive luxuriance of some tropical swamp, possibly in Java. He wondered where Light was: it was almost certainly checking its location using the data banks in the spaceship. Through the chorus of insects, he fancied he heard the scuttering of information across the ship's screens. Nonsense, of course – they were much too high. The important thing was to find Control before she fell into the wrong clutches.

Light stood in the hall and stared up at the stained glass window over the stairs. Data symbols flickered across its surface, hierographics and hologlyphics like those the Doctor had seen on the screens in the ship. No, this could not be the Earth. If it was, the implications were too momentious to contemplate, so let the idea be.

Repeatedly, the screen identified the location: Earth. 'Ecosphere data assessment completed. Amendments to original subject fields required.' Impossible! The Earth was far from the ship's prescribed course. Either Control or the Survey Agent had disturbed the ship's perceptions and caused some minor error in its location relays. They would be severely punished once this was rectified.

Light was Light. Who or what it was, it never stopped to recall. Who knew where its work had started? It was not to be found on its catalogue. Record all life – perhaps it had thought of its directive itself. Species were what it recorded, not what it was! Every species, every subspecies and every variant was noted and neatly, logically recorded. It must know every change, every variegated mutation. The catalogue must be complete and up to date, but why did it never stop? It needed just one hiatus, a few moments to catch up; time to breathe, time to think. There was no time to waste: there were corrections and amendments. Never a moment to halt, to combat the weariness that layered and dulled the play of energetics that was his mind, was Light.

The screen reiterated, 'Location: Earth.'

One of the dominant creatures of this planet was approaching. Light regarded her, a tall and proud specimen in black. The form that the Survey Agent would have taken might not be dissimilar to this. Mrs Pritchard bobbed and held out a silver platter upon which a card rested.

Was this a challenge? Light had no need to examine the card to understand its purport.

'From Mr Josiah, sir. An invitation to dinner,' said the housekeeper.

So the Survey Agent was well established. Had Light not seen it already? It contemplated a response while Mrs Pritchard waited, stoney-faced, lit by its lambent aura. It watched a beetle drop from a curtain rail and lie on its back, legs waving helplessly. It nodded in agreement.

'Dinner will be served at half past eight, sir.' Mrs

Pritchard bobbed again and departed, leaving Light to its facts and figures on the screen above.

'Location: Earth,' the screen stated again. Light's energy droned angrily.

A moment later a maid entered the hall carrying a tray and large soup tureen. She stopped short as she caught Light's eye.

'Come child, I have need of your services.'

It beckoned and she drew near, trustingly returning his gaze. Since the ship's conclusions were nonsense, Light must find out where this place was for itself. The maid knelt as if to receive benediction, staring up into Light's cold angelic face. The tray began to rattle as Light enfolded her in the cloak of its aura.

The distant clatter of a fallen tureen echoed through the night chorus of insects. Ace grabbed the Doctor's arm. 'What was that?'

'Just our imaginations,' he said. They had not gone much further, and there was still no sign of Control. The place crawled with all manner of life.

'The energy from Light's ship is doing this,' she said.

The Doctor took a deep breath. 'Yes. Invigorating, isn't it?'

'No.'

'Why? What does it remind you of?' He saw he was about to get a piece of her mind, so he undercut her flow. 'All right, all right. What happened to you here in a hundred years' time is none of my business.'

'I thought it was a haunted house,' she protested.

'It is.'

'I got frightened, that's all!'

'Of course.'

'I was only fourteen!'

As he looked at her with deep affection, she understood that he was trying to apologize.

The Doctor took the key to the TARDIS from his pocket and offered it to her. 'You can always wait for me.'

'That's the easy way out,' she said sharply.

131

'Well, come on then,' he said, but she was too fascinated to hear. The passage was engendering a lure of its own. She heard shadows whispering and scrabbling as they clustered in the corners. She froze. 'Doctor? Did you ever have one of those nightmares where you couldn't move?'

No answer: he had gone.

She felt the raw energy of hatred fixing on her, making her the eye of its storm. There in the shadows, it was watching her; the core of all the rotting rot in rotten Perivale. This was where it all started to go wrong. Families and mums and mum's fancy man. And she had let it go on. She should have stopped it properly. All the hatred and guilt in the world was concentrated in this place. She was trapped a hundred years from where she should be, where she should have saved her friend.

The scrabbling and whispering surged closer. All around her the insects mocked: the place was alive. A raven croaked and Ace threw out her arms to shield herself. An owl screeched. The beady eyes of the frozen birds accused her as she tried to run, but her legs were heavy as lead. This way and that she turned, beset by the screaming judgment of the lifeless birds. She sank to the floor weeping uncontrollably.

'You're all dead! I didn't mean it! I couldn't help it! I'm not guilty!' As she buried her face in her hands, she heard the sirens of the fire engines approaching and saw the flashing blue beacons of the next century cutting through the smoke and blazing firelight.

It all went quiet. Behind her, Ace heard the rustle of material. She looked round and for a second saw Manisha standing over her.

'Ace, my dear,' said the apparition. 'I want you to come away. Come away with me to Java!' Raising her chloroform-drenched pad, Gwendoline launched herself upon Ace with murderous intent.

11

Trick of the Light

Inspector Mackenzie's search for a way out of the house had proved fruitless. The outer doors were all sealed; every window on the ground floor was either barred or shuttered. The telephone line was dead and the kitchen was empty. Mrs Grose had departed long ago without leaving any dinner cooking. The inspector found some biscuits in the pantry and decided that he must find a way down from an upstairs window. That might prove tricky because his joints ached as if they had not been used for a week, but he was not staying in this houseful of lunatics for a moment longer than was necessary.

As he reached the hall, he saw Lady Margaret, still dressed as a housekeeper, overseeing the packing of a set of trunks by two of the maids. Evidently preparations were under way for a departure. As each item was displayed, she ticked it off in a notebook and consigned it to a trunk.

'Item: one machete. To be dispatched with other sundries to the lodgings in Wigmore Street.

'Item: three revolvers. As required.'

She noticed Mackenzie watching and fixed him with her stare.

'Ah, Lady Margaret,' he blustered, 'I've been wanting to have a word with you.'

The housekeeper snapped her fingers and the two maids started to close in on the policeman.

'Perhaps we can sort this business out over a pot of tea.'

He glanced from one to the other of the maids as they took hold of his arms.

'Item,' said Mrs Pritchard. 'One police inspector. This specimen to be packed with other items for London.' She ticked her notebook.

With a shout, Mackenzie flung his handful of biscuits into her face, wrenched himself free of the startled maids and ran up the stairs.

'Doctor!' he yelled.

Mrs Pritchard took the machete from the trunk and handed it to one of the maids.

'Dispose of that item,' she said.

She watched the maids set off after their quarry. One of her staff was dead, another missing. Whatever Mr Josiah's plans for the inspector were, a housekeeper was entitled to exact revenge for the disturbance of her house. She closed the trunk lid and went to see about dinner.

It had not been difficult for the Doctor to find Control's trail: he had only to follow the scattered rags and veils to realize that her evolutionary progress was advancing rapidly. Thankfully, it had not been a trail of husks: Control seemed to have out-evolved Josiah as far as metamorphosis was concerned. She was butterfly and chrysalis in one. The problem would lie in not frightening her away again. And now Ace had wandered off, which annoyed him.

Through the crack around the half-open door to Gwendoline's bedroom, he saw that Control had found a new ally. Redvers Fenn-Cooper sat on the rumpled bed, holding some picture or other, which he was examining studiously. The Doctor wondered for a moment who the handsome young woman seated at the dressing-table amid a stack of opened hat boxes could be. Her less than elegant manner gave the game away, as she planted an elaborately feathered hat on to her piled honey-coloured hair. The hat was at entirely the wrong angle and Control growled a little.

Without looking up from his picture, Redvers observed, 'The handsomest woman Redvers ever saw was daughter to an N'tamba chief. But she had a bone through her nose and ate her cousin for breakfast.'

Control threw down the hat and selected another with stiff gauze and a stuffed swallow on the brim. The Doctor considered whether her filthy rags had evolved into the charming mauve dress she now wore, or whether she and Redvers had chosen it between them.

'Will Control be a ladylike?' she pleaded, gazing at her new reflection. 'Want so much!'

She discarded the hat again, but Redvers, having put down his painting, approached and stood behind her. Picking up the necklace he had given her, he gently draped it around her neck and fastened the clasp.

'Once the hunt is over, I'll make you the finest ladylike in the Empire,' he said in admiration.

He sat back on the bed and returned to his picture, offering the Doctor the ideal opportunity to make an entrance.

'Hallo, Control. Having fun?' he said genially, swanning through the door.

Control spun round in alarm, hissing venomously at the intruder. 'You!' she cried. 'You come taking away Control's freeness!'

'No, Control,' he said as she backed off. 'I want to help you. And I need your help too!'

'No help!' she snarled and thrust him away. 'Freeness is mine! You won't take it!' She had had enough of this world. She turned and hurled herself through the glass of the window.

The Doctor dashed after her, yelling through the cascade of splinters for her to come back; she couldn't get far. But he only glimpsed her down below, dashing off into the darkness, away from the house and the Light.

Redvers looked up from his picture and said, 'Of course, if she were a real lady, I wouldn't be in her boudoir.'

'Things are getting out of hand,' despaired the Doctor. 'Even I can't play this many games at once.'

'Then help me. You can join my hunt,' suggested the explorer.

'I don't have time, Redvers.' The Doctor had an uncomfortable feeling that lost overnight in the dark, Control might evolve into a nocturnal creature and never come back inside again.

'But I'm hunting the rarest creature in the world. The Crowned Saxe-Coburg!' Redvers handed his picture to the Doctor, who looked in astonishment but wasn't a bit surprised. He was holding a picture of Queen Victoria with a set of target rings and bullet punctures across her regal brow.

'Oh, really? And who's sponsoring this expedition? Josiah Samuel Smith?' He might have known that this was where Josiah would set his sights. He was programmed to evolve into one of the planet's dominant lifeforms, but why stop there when he might have the throne as well. Crowned Saxe-Coburg indeed! Of course, Josiah would block the truth from Redvers' bewildered mind, but to adapt Mrs Saxe-Coburg – a nickname from the lowest reaches of society – into a totem within Redvers' domain, questioned not only Josiah's sick humour but also the company he kept. Perhaps he already had contacts in London.

With Control beyond reach, the Doctor decided his attention was best employed here and in finding Ace. And the biggest problem was going to be dealing with Light, whatever it was up to.

Redvers took back the picture of Victoria Regina and said, 'When I find it, I shall shoot it!'

Nimrod knew he had found Light when he saw a steady stream of golden haze emanating beneath the door of the Trophy room. He had so many questions, and if the wise men spoke with the voice of the god when questioned, then surely the god himself was wiser still. For all that Josiah had taught Nimrod, it was Light, the Burning One, who had brought him to this tamed, unwild place. Would he not also take him home? But Light had questions and apprehensions of his own.

As Nimrod entered, he saw his God bent over the maid, who was laid out on the dissecting bench. Light turned to stare at the newcomer and in its hand, it held the maid's detached arm, bloodily severed at the shoulder.

'I wanted to see how it worked,' it said, 'so I dismantled it.' Its cold stare settled on Nimrod's own wondering eyes. 'But I need another specimen . . .'

Nimrod bowed his head. 'Sir, you are Light. Long ago, my people worshipped you as the Burning One.

The pupils of Light's eyes narrowed. 'I know you. I took you up as the last specimen of the extinct Neanderthal race from Earth.'

'Yes, sir.'

'At least they knew when to stop evolving. Who released you from your quarantine cubicle?'

'Mr Josiah, sir. I am in his service.'

That name again, undoubtedly the evolved form of the Survey Agent. Still, here was a specimen that Light could discourse with. It pointed a finger into the air and teased the molecules so that they flared into visibility, spinning in a glowing orb before it.

'Look at these microbes. They're evolving even as I speak! If this is Earth, my entire catalogue of the planet is worthless! Centuries of work wasted!'

It flicked its finger and the orb disintegrated into the air.

Nimrod tried to take in the god's words, but all he could perceive were the cold eyes and the callous, empty voice. His people revered the state of mind that others called madness, but Light was beyond this different sanity. Nimrod realized with mounting fear that his god was destructively and monstrously unhinged.

The door opened and Mackenzie appeared, out of breath and red in the face. Seeing Nimrod, he gasped, 'Thank heavens. Safe at last. That mad woman's after me. She's . . .' he faltered as Light emerged from behind Nimrod's shoulder.

'And if we don't want things to change,' it said, 'we make sure that they cannot!'

Mackenzie fell backwards against the door as all colour drained from him. Under the stare, he began to sink slowly to the floor, choking and frothing, his eyes streaming with rich dark tears.

Ace knew enough about fights to easily hold her own against a genteel Victorian miss, but she was in a state of nervous shock and Gwendoline had the strength of a Turkish wrestler. Ace caught her first whiff of chloroform and fought like a demon. Screwing her eyes shut, she kicked and bit for all she was worth. Gwendoline stumbled and Ace ran blindly away down the passage, crushing insects underfoot. She wanted to find the Doctor, but instinct drew her towards the TARDIS.

As she hurtled around a corner, a maid stepped out in her path. Gwendoline was right behind her and Ace had no choice but to dart through a door into another disused bedroom. She tried to force the door shut, but Gwendoline was already pushing it in and the maid had joined her.

'Come along Ace, I don't want to hurt you,' called Gwendoline.

'You mean it'll be painless!' retaliated Ace. But with nothing to jam against the handle, she was gradually losing the battle. With a hefty shove, Gwendoline forced her way into the room. The maid stood in the doorway watching as the two girls fought like cats. Then, hearing voices, she darted back into the passage, closing the door behind her.

'The Crowned Saxe-Coburg's habitat isn't easy to discover,' Redvers was telling the Doctor, as they rounded the corner.

'A good hunter always knows the signs,' the Doctor agreed. The maid, who stood in the doorway smiling, bobbed dutifully as they passed. Redvers eyed her warily, as he remembered something Redvers had once told him: the ready smile of a native may well be that of a crocodile. But the Doctor continued, '. . . signs, like a royal invitation to Windsor Castle for instance.' He stopped, looked sternly at Redvers and held out his hand.

The explorer resolutely shook his head.

'Come on, Redvers,' pressed the Doctor. 'Access to the

royaal family. Why else would Josiah keep you alive so long?

With a sigh, Redvers produced a battered envelope with a royal seal on it. He held it back for a moment. 'Actually, it's for Buckingham Palace. A reception.' Finally, he shrugged and handed it over. 'After all, you are a member of the Royal Geographical Society.'

The Doctor held the envelope for a second and then passed it back.

Redvers smiled gratefully. 'Will you join my expedition, Doctor?'

'Not yet,' he said, setting off at a pace. 'First I have to find Ace.'

The maid watched them disappear. She released her grip on the door-handle and waited, listening to the muffled sounds of the struggle from the room.

Ace had Gwendoline in a head lock, but there was no where to secure the vicious little Victorian and no one to help her do it. Gwendoline tried to kick Ace's shins, but her long skirts hampered her movements.

'Let go of me, you little brat!' she cried out, still trying to reach Ace's face with her pad.

'No way!' Behind her, Ace heard the rumble of the window sliding up. As if in answer to a prayer, a hand appeared, clad in a lady's long and grubby evening glove. Control, her hair dishevelled, her eyes wild and her will broken, hauled herself in through the gap.

'Control! Help me!' shouted Ace, but the creature only stared at the struggle and muttered, 'Poor Control. No hoping. No changing,' in a voice bereft of all energy.

'Oh, yeah! What about poor Ace? Well, help me, why don't you!'

Control moved forward and thrust them both out of her way, allowing Gwendoline to break free. She rounded on Ace again, but Control had pulled open the door and seized hold of the maid. The startled woman was sent careering into Gwendoline and they both collapsed in a heap.

Ace dashed out into the passage after Control, slamming the door behind her and turning the key in the lock. From inside came Gwendoline's most unladylike curse, followed by a sharp slap as she took out her spite on the unfortunate maid's face.

The door-handle began to rattle; blows started to pound on the panelling. Control had gone by now, but Ace cared only about finding the Doctor. She just wanted to get out and she wasn't worried whether she saw any of the others again: not Control nor Josiah nor any of his mad family; not Mackenzie nor Nimrod nor Light – especially not Light.

Josiah stalked the upper observatory, rapidly losing patience at the lack of any news. He had tried the telephone, but as he lifted it a beetle had crawled from the earpiece. He threw down the receiver in disgust. When he tried again, the line was dead.

A few minutes later, Nimrod came up the stairs.

'Where's Redvers?' demanded Josiah. 'I told you to fetch him back.'

Nimrod had a determined air that Josiah disliked. 'My circumstances have changed, sir. I wish to serve notice of the termination of my employment.'

This was laughable. 'What? Without me you have nothing!' But suddenly Josiah was afraid. He snatched up his pistol, held it to Nimrod's temples and forced the manservant to his knees. 'What's Light been saying to you? Or that Doctor? I know where your true allegiance lies!'

Defying the barrel of the gun, Nimrod rose to his feet and declared, 'With myself, sir.'

With a look of utter contempt, Josiah pushed his servant away. 'Where are the others?' he cried. 'It's almost dinner time. Why aren't they all dead?' With a final glare at Nimrod, he disappeared down into the house. 'Do I have to do everything myself!'

Light stood watching, its hand stroking the side of the TARDIS. It studied one of the observatory's arched windows and the darkness beyond. 'I think I shall be late for dinner,' it mused.

* * *

Ace was certain that the Doctor was nearby, watching her. If this was another of his games . . . She had come back round the house close to Gwendoline's room and as she reached the door, she thought she heard someone crying.

There was a momentary flare of white outside the window as if a minor comet had just fizzed past the house. Then it was gone.

Ace looked warily into the room and saw a shape crouched on the floor, enveloped in an eiderdown. She approached the shape and called gently, 'Control?'

The shape tensed. 'Go way! Leave lone!' it snapped.

Ace sat down on the floor beside it. 'Am I still Ratkin?' she asked. Control wailed miserably, so Ace tried to put her arm around where she supposed the shape's shoulders might be. 'I didn't mean it. It's all right.'

'Hate world!' snivelled Control. 'Hate freeness! It bites! Ran away into big empty nothing. Sky flew away to nothing! No freeness. No changing. Crawl back. Want to hide from big open emptiness world!'

Ace shook her head in agreement. 'It's this house. When you're a kid, you smash things you hate. But what do I do if it keeps coming back?'

They were united in misery. 'World only changing for him,' whined Control. 'Now he's Josiah. Big man now! Leaving Control behind! No ladylike!' She erupted into a wail of such anguish that Ace couldn't stand it any more.

'Cut the whingeing, Control!' she ordered and the cry stopped as quickly as a baby discovering a new toy. 'You want to fight back? You'll have to beat Josiah at his own game!'

Control's head emerged, wide-eyed and alert from the eiderdown. For the first time, Ace comprehended the extent of her frantic evolution; she looked almost human.

As Ace went and hunted through a stack of books by the squirrel's doll's house, Control discarded her eiderdown and watched in fascination. Ace came back with *Etiquette for the Modern Lady* by S A Mayhew-Archer. 'I dunno how long we've got, but we can make a start.'

'Hey!' she protested, as Control snatched the book out of

her hands. The creature sniffed the binding and opened the first pages.

'Other way up,' advised Ace, realizing this was going to be a long job.

'This make Control ladylike?' asked the pupil.

'How many years have you got?'

'Not long.' Control held the book up against her forehead. For a few seconds, she hummed a continuous rising note to herself and shuddered. Then she lowered the book, breathed a sigh of relief, smiled and threw the book away. 'Done, done,' she said proudly.

'Oh, what! No one absorbs a whole book of information just like that,' thought Ace.

'Not just no one,' said Control and winked. She sat in front of the mirror and started to tidy her hair. Ace was still incredulous. It was a pity there was no chapter on elocution.

'Go on. Say after me. "The rain in Spain falls mainly down the drain".'

'The rain . . . in Spain . . . ,' Control began in less than perfect tones, but stopped as she saw a movement behind her in the mirror.

'There you are at last, Ace my dear!' sneered Gwendoline.

She lunged forward with her pad, but Ace caught her arm and forced her sideways. Snatching out, she tore Gwendoline's locket from her neck and threw it down.

As the two grappled again, toppling headlong onto the bed, Control called excitedly from the ringside, 'New gameplay? Control go next!'

'It can be arranged!' shouted Gwendoline, overpowering Ace and bringing the chloroform pad down on her face.

There was a scramble of activity as Redvers burst into the room. He dragged the screaming Gwendoline away from Ace and held her struggling. 'The natives are restless tonight, Doctor!' he commented.

Shaking off the effects of the vapour, Ace saw the Doctor scoop the locket off the floor and open it up. 'Look at this, Gwendoline,' he said, showing her the contents. 'Who does it remind you of?'

The girl gasped and stopped struggling. She stared at the twin portraits in their gold frames: one of a proud and beautiful woman in her mid-forties; the other, a doe-eyed young girl untouched by thoughts of the world's wicked ways. The pictures were of Lady Margaret Pritchard and her daughter, Gwendoline.

The Doctor gently sat the blank-faced girl on the bed. 'Severe trauma,' he diagnosed. 'I might forgive her arranging trips to Java . . .'

'She was hypnotized, Doctor,' advised Redvers.

'. . . if she didn't enjoy it so much.'

Gwendoline sat motionless like a discarded doll. The Doctor snapped the locket shut and pocketed it. 'Ace? I see you've made a friend.'

'Don't ask,' muttered Ace. 'Control has a few things to show Josiah.'

Control stepped forward proudly. 'No longer hiding!' she announced.

The Doctor smiled. He knew he was right to have let Ace deal with this problem. From the depths of the house, a gong sounded. 'Good. Just in time for dinner.' He held out his arm and Control graciously took it. With Ace and Redvers following, he escorted Control down to dinner.

12
Beautiful Soup

A dark tapestry of fields and woodland was lit by the rising
moon. The stone edifice of Gabriel Chase dwindled into the
darkness as Light flew like a spinning meteor across the
sky. Here and there, groups of dwellings clustered in the
valleys where the dominant species, omnivorous like swine,
set up their colonies. More than that, Light felt the endless
motion and change of existence that it knew from many a
world; yet in the whole universe, only one planet harboured
such an abundance of multifarious life. Earth, as Light
loathed to recall, also had a single empty satellite moon.

Light thought its flight faster, east towards the oncoming
track of the sun. It raced the silver rope of a river, cutting
through a great cityspread that smothered nature's growth
on its banks. Rows of lamps twinkled among the reeking
chimneys. Carriages and engines trundled up and down
their bustling courses. There was the smell of rusting iron
and stagnant water. Yet even here, plants forced their way
between the cracks, animals scurried through the waste-
pipes and insects bred in the rotting heaps of refuse. And
in the darkest gullies and alleys, the weakest humanesque
denizens of the city huddled together in the filth for
warmth, clutching their starving infants which squealed
their right to survive.

Thinking itself even faster, Light's path seared through
swirls of flying insects and disturbed the swifts that slept
on the wing. Far below, it saw the river spread wide into

the sea. As it guessed, the water teemed with organisms of every genera through surface plankton and myriad shoals of fish to worms that squirmed in the slime deep below. And these last creatures had not changed, not since the first time they were catalogued how many thousands of years ago?

With growing anger, Light sped beyond the edge of the mountainous seas and over the forests, crags and plains of a vast continent. Faster and faster its mind raced, but it knew by now. As it saw the first glow of the rising sun advancing to meet it over the Pacific, its thoughts turned back to Gabriel Chase.

In a flash of radiance that set the window blinds spinning, Light returned, filling the upper observatory with the angry drone of its aura. Nimrod saw its massive shape reform, as it folded back its liquid gold cloak like vast wings. Within the glow, its image trembled slightly, as if it now held only the most tenuous grip on its shape and its sanity.

With disgust, it whispered, 'It's still changing. Seething with life! Every plane and crevice crawls with it! It's never ceased changing, evolving. But I still know the stench of its overripe, infested carcass. This is Earth. And it has seen its last day!'

Josiah looked at his gold hunter pocket-watch. Mrs Pritchard had correctly laid only three places for dinner, but Gwendoline was late and so was the guest.

The housekeeper and her two remaining servants waited by the red walls of the dining room. When Mrs Pritchard had entered the kitchen and found nothing prepared for the evening meal, she had come close to panic. She returned to the dining room and was astonished to discover that a tureen of dark brown soup had already been set on the table. There was no time to question its origins, but this was not the service to her master that she prided herself on. She consoled herself with a dark suspicion that dinner would not last beyond the first course. She was a loyal servant, but if Josiah was destroyed, surely the house would remain. Would that mean any more for her than a simple change of masters?

Light would come soon. It had accepted Josiah's invitation. It needed him. And he could brazen it out. He was human now. The innumerable forms, in which he, the Survey Agent, had catalogued innumerable worlds for Light, were things of the past. Earth was where he belonged. He had evolved to his own requirements, not Light's: he was a self-made man. To hell with Control and Light, he had outgrown their triangle. Lure them back into the ship and be rid of them once and for all. With so much to live for, he knew he could succeed. Time and time again he convinced himself of it. Light would soon come.

There was a noise from the drawing room. Josiah readied himself to meet his guest.

'Good evening, Josiah,' said the Doctor, with a knowing grin. He escorted Control to the table, saw the tureen and hissed to Ace, who had entered with Redvers, 'Don't touch the soup.'

Josiah saw Control and exploded with anger. 'Get that creature out of here! Get it out!'

The Doctor firmly guided Control to a place at the table. 'Go on Control, knock 'em dead!' muttered Ace.

Control looked proudly across at Josiah and enunciated in sedate but gravelly tones. 'Control has her freeness now, squire.'

Ace cheered. 'Yeah! I knew you could do it!'

The knuckles of Josiah's fists whitened with anger. 'What's this?' he demanded.

'I'm surprised you remember Control,' said the Doctor. 'It's so long since you had her locked up.'

'Where's Gwendoline?' Josiah had endured enough insults from uninvited guests. But before the Doctor could answer, Control cut in. 'Better orf without you, guv'nor!'

Ace giggled, but Josiah levelled a finger at the real cause of his predicament. 'You win this move Doctor, but I will not suffer that animal at my table!'

Redvers had remained silent until now, but there were limits beyond which discourtesy could not be stretched.

'That, sir, is no way to speak in front of a ladylike,' he warned.

Josiah looked startled at this reprimand and Ace, loving every minute of the tyrant's humiliation, chipped in, 'Oi, Jungle Jim, I'm here too, you know.'

Control nodded graciously to Redvers and reassured her champion, 'No one hurting Control. Control looking after self, thanking you. Not in gutter now!' The last remark was aimed at Josiah, who scowled poisonously.

'Who was it who said Earthmen never invite their ancestors round for dinner?' pondered the Doctor. He slipped from his place and approached Mrs Pritchard, who had been puzzling over the difference in numbers of places set for dinner and guests who had arrived.

'Lady Pritchard,' he said and saw a momentary flicker of recognition in her eyes. He fished the locket from his jacket and handed it to her. 'I found this. I think it's your daughter Gwendoline's, but it's got your portrait in too. You see?'

Lady Margaret's hardened glare seemed to thaw as she gazed at the sepia portraits in their frames. She stepped back in confusion as a long-bolted door in her corridored mind suddenly swung wide open and let in the air and the light. She once had a daughter. Perhaps still . . .

'Quite a resemblance,' added the Doctor. 'You and Sir George must have had a happy family before the cuckoo invaded your nest.'

A single forgotten, frozen tear melted in her eye. 'Gwendoline,' she choked. And worst of all, she had bolted the cold, dark door on her memories herself. She ran from the room.

'Mrs Pritchard!' yelled Josiah. 'You are not dismissed!'

Redvers retaliated instinctively. 'Let her go, sir. The lioness always protects her cubs.'

Ace had leaned forward to stir the contents of the tureen. Something glinted in the brown liquid.

'No soup, Ace!' reprimanded the Doctor. She dropped the ladle.

147

'There's no way out of this for you, Doctor!' warned Josiah.

The Doctor was unruffled. 'Oh, I knew it was a trap as soon as I walked into it.' He indicated the empty place at the far end of the table. 'Unfortunately, your guest of honour seems to have let you down.'

'You've been blown out,' jeered Ace. 'Too bad.'

With a smack, Josiah brought a silver serving spoon down on an iridescent goliath beetle that was crossing the table. 'Light will come,' he said.

Instinct drew Lady Margaret up through the house to her daughter's bedroom. She found a young woman there, sitting forlornly on the bed, but one look at the portrait confirmed that this was indeed her daughter. She called Gwendoline's name, but there was no response. A feeling of maternal irritation came over her. 'Silly girl, I warned you not to play in here,' she scolded.

Gwendoline blinked several times as if in waking. She slowly turned and looked at the woman who had been her servant. Her mouth opened as she tried to mouth the word 'Mamma'.

Her mother fell forward and embraced the child. For long moments they clung to each other, reunited after so long so close, yet so monstrously distant.

Lady Margaret stroked Gwendoline's hair, memories welling in her mind. She was so afraid of losing the past again; so afraid of returning to the present.

'We were so happy once. Remember riding with your father down to the village. And the dogs running behind the carriage, barking. But then your father went away to Java. You sent him.'

Gwendoline clung tightly to her mother. At last, through the tears, the words came. 'Mamma! I thought you were lost!'

Lady Margaret knelt before her daughter and clasped her hands. 'I am, dear. We both are.' But it seemed so far away now. It faded in the golden haze that was spreading dreamlike through the room.

'Oh, Mamma. What have we done?'

'You changed,' said Light. He was scrutinizing them with distaste from across the bedroom. 'Like the rest of this verminous planet, you adapted to your new situation to survive.'

Pierced by the crazed, analytical eyes of the angel of retribution, their minds grew numb and heavy. Their limbs lost all will to move. Their pale skins whitened and hardened, crackling as they succumbed to a creeping, grey hoar-frost.

Nimrod came through the door, drawn by the radiance, and faltered in his tracks. Seated on and beside the bed were two perfect statues of Lady Margaret Pritchard and her daughter Gwendoline, their reunion preserved, for-wever calcified in stone.

'They never harmed you,' said the manservant.

'I have decided Earth's future,' declared the angel. 'Follow me to dinner.'

Nimrod was instantly alone. Although he was trapped in the wrong time and place perhaps, he knew that this was the world he still belonged to. He had changed, but he was still the tale-bearer; he still carried the past with him. Now he might even write the tales he bore as words in books for the whole world to read. None of it must be lost, not his past, his people's past, nor even the whole world's. But unless Light was stopped, it would all be gone for ever. His head full of desperate thoughts, he ran from the room.

Josiah sat at the head of his table, tapping out the seconds with his knife on the crystal stem of his wine glass. He awaited an invited guest who did not appear, surrounded by guests he did not welcome. Well, when Light came, he would feed the others to it, one by one, and then it would see he had not been idle and he would trick it into his power and trap it, even extinguish its cold, heartless heart and then . . .

'So Josiah, tell me about your plan to assassinate Queen Victoria,' said the Doctor, leaning back in his chair, opposite his host.

'Your what!' exclaimed Ace.

An icy spasm of fear turned in Josiah's stomach. 'Who have you been talking to!' He threw a sudden glance of accusation at Redvers, who looked up startled from the napkin he had been studiously folding into a crown.

'Myself mainly,' the Doctor confessed. 'But to be honest, you're not really Empire material, are you? I mean, your background's a bit dodgy. And I doubt if Light'll be amused.'

'Neither'll Queen Vic,' inserted Ace.

Josiah lounged back arrogantly. 'The British Empire?' he scoffed. 'It's an anarchic mess! There's no clear directive from the throne! No discipline! Result – confusion, wastage. I can provide a new order – wealth, prosperity . . .'

The Doctor had heard it all before. '. . . confusion, wastage, tyranny, burnt toast, until all the atlas is pink!' He hummed a snatch of Rule Britannia and saluted. 'But it isn't your invitation to Buckingham Palace. Redvers!'

He sat back confidently, having poured the fat into the fire. Now let others play the roles he had rehearsed in his mind. Redvers rose on cue and taking the envelope from his pocket, slowly paced around the table. 'I am allowed to take a guest,' he said.

Josiah reached out expectantly, but Redvers moved on past him towards Control, who rose hardly daring to believe. 'Control's proper ladylike now,' she said, her voice trembling slightly. 'Out to dinner. Take Control meeting Queen lady.'

Redvers' handsome, grizzled features smiled at her, but a hand came snaking over his shoulder and Josiah's voice crooned into his ear. 'Redvers. We agreed. We hunt the Crowned Saxe-Coburg together.'

Redvers moved the envelope clear of the grasping hand and shook his head apologetically. 'I gave up on Redvers long ago. All he ever talks about is himself!'

He looked into Control's eyes. She was the first thing he had seen clearly for heaven knows how long. All the rest were phantasms and mirages, brought about by too long alone in the interior. 'Here, Control,' he said and gave her the invitation.

Ace saw Control take the envelope and Josiah lunge forward to tear it from her. 'Give me that letter!' he cried in anguish. Every move imprinted itself in detail on Ace's mind, as if all time was slowly tumbling inwards on her. She suddenly knew that something terrible would happen.

Control snatched the envelope clear, but the maids began to move in from the walls towards her. 'It's mine,' she shouted, 'or I burn it!' With one movement, she swung round and held the battered invitation towards the fireplace.

Ace saw the flames reaching up, eager for the paper. Just a stray spark could set it alight, or a match thrown by a frightened kid, whose flame unchecked could flower into a blazing inferno. Fire would lick along dry frames and timbers; black, choking wood-smoke would fill the house and the stone's would crack in the heat.

Josiah moved slowly towards Control. 'You basest of creatures! You dare to defy me! I am a man of property!'

'Then I burn whole house up!' Control thrust the precious envelope over the flames. Josiah choked: he was unable to move lest it should drop.

Ace could hold back no longer. 'No, Control! Don't do it! That's what I did in 1983! Please! Don't do it again!'

The Doctor caught her in his arms. This was not what he had rehearsed in his head. 'Ace. You didn't tell me.'

'You're not my probation officer! You don't have to know everything!'

Oh, how he sometimes wished that was true. 'Ace.' He cradled her gently.

'The whole house was full of evil and hate left by him!' She pointed at Josiah, whose eyes had never left the slowly singeing invitation. 'This house! So I burnt it down! I had to!' She buried her head in the Doctor's embrace.

Control, absorbing every word of Ace's confession as she met Josiah's hateful stare, said simply, 'It is wickedness,' and dropped the envelope into the fire.

'No!' Josiah scrabbled in the hearth to retrieve the burning invitation, but a wave of radiance that filled the whole dining room carried it out of his fingers. It spiralled in the heat, away up the chimney.

The Doctor gently rocked Ace and hushed her tears. 'It's all right, Ace. That's that. He only wanted to take over the Empire. At least he didn't want to destroy the world.' It was only then that he noticed the flow of radiance and the incessant, angry drone of Light's aura.

Light stood at the head of the table in the host's place, like a golden, vulturine messenger of death seeking its carrion. For the moment, it seemed more concerned with the tureen of lukewarm soup than with the company assembled in its presence.

'Light. I think I've solved your problem for you,' the Doctor began optimistically.

'There's only one solution to the Earth,' it intoned.

Ace, the thoughts of her own drama driven away by the extraordinary focus of the angel, again saw something glinting in the tureen. On some impulse, she saw her hand reach out and stir the ladle.

Josiah stepped obsequiously forward. 'Light, the survey of this planet is complete,' he fawned. 'It is ready for your examination.'

Apparently Light did not hear. 'I was going to reduce it to this,' it said, watching as Ace raised the ladle. Dangling from it was the medallion of a Victorian police inspector.

'So you started with Inspector Mackenzie,' observed the Doctor.

Ace dropped the spoon and turned away repulsed. From beside the fireplace came Josiah's laughter. 'The cream of Scotland Yard!'

With a nod, the Doctor concurred, 'The most precious substance in the univers: primordial soup, from which all life springs.'

The tureen slid along the table towards Light and the ladle swivelled round into the angel's outstretched hand. It raised the spoon and watched the soup trickling slowly back into the dish. A scum of bubbles had begun to form on the glossy brown surface of the liquor.

'Merely sugars, proteins and amino acids . . . But it would soon evolve again. It's already starting.'

Light's voice had a quietness that was too controlled, too ethereally calm. But the illusion was spoiled by the alarming burr of its aura. Its finger stabbed down.

'But I'll stop the change here. All organic life will be eradicated in the firestorm. I'll leave the archaeologists a simple, sterile, charred cinder to puzzle over. And when this world is destroyed . . . No more change. Never again. No more evolution. No more life.' It dipped its finger into the turgid brown soup. 'No more amendments to my catalogue.' It sucked the coating of greasy liquor from its finger and smiled with satisfaction.

The Doctor was forced to observe Light objectively. It was the only way to restrain his anger at its final solution. The creature, force or phenomenon, what ever it was, had no physical rest mass but it did have pressure. As a mind, it existed on the brink of insanity, he was sure of that; its catalogue was the obsession that had driven it there. That might have started as a work of love, but if Light was as old as this universe, the rich diversity of its work had become an unrelenting task and then a tortuous, grinding labour; it could never be relinquished. There would always be more new subjects to catalogue. It could never cease while the superstrings of existence grew ever more diverse. Madness in so awesome a creature meant that more than one world would get hurt: Earth would be only the first planet crushed by Light's frenzied wings. Searching frantically for a defence, the Doctor saw only one alternative to Light's antagonized fury of revenge and that was cold despair.

'You evolve too, Light,' he said quietly.

'Nonsense!' Light's voice immediately took on an edge. At the heart of the aura, the image of the angel tremored slightly. The Doctor felt the full concentrated force of its analytical scrutiny.

'Of course you do. All the time you adapt and change: your attitude, your place, your mind. Just look at you now. That's not your original shape.'

153

Ace could only watch the showdown. Light loomed over the Doctor, its eyes darting in confusion. The monstrous presence was clumsy and unimaginative compared with the quiet goading of its adversary, but it still might crush him in a fit of pique.

'I don't think much of your catalogue either,' added the Doctor. 'It's full of gaps.'

'All organic life is recorded!' Light threw an angry glance at Josiah, who swallowed hard.

The Doctor sniffed dismissively. 'Then where are the griffins and the basilisks? You missed the dragons and bandersnatches!'

Light's aura died away, or retracted, leaving the bitter cold shape of the angel like a silvered husk staring as the Doctor backed out through the doorway. The prospect of yet more subjects to index and more errors to correct deadened its weary soul.

'And what about the slithy toves and the Crowned Saxe-Coburg?'

The tormentor's voice faded down the passage leading to the hall, where Light was already scanning its chattering index on the stained-glass window.

'Where are these items!'

Really Light was pretty dim. It had about as much imagination as a pocket calculator. 'I can't think how you missed them,' goaded the Doctor. 'You must complete the catalogue before you destroy all life here.'

Streams of data began to spill from the area of the window screen across the walls and into the air. 'Control!' shouted Light. It could force the rebellious creature to supply the answers.

'She's no good to you any more,' needled the Doctor. 'She's evolved as well!'

Light snarled and the relentless data chattered louder around it, pressing in on its mind like the voices of all the teeming life on this vile, infested planet. 'No! All slipping away!'

The Doctor leaned nonchalantly against the banisters and asked, 'Excuse me, Light, but weren't you in the dining

154

room just now? You haven't changed your location, have you?'

He braced himself as Light's trembling head turned to fix him with its deadly stare, but the nerve-jangling pulse of the data drew its gaze back to the screen. 'What's the matter, Light? Change your mind again?' he taunted.

'You are endlessly agitating, unceasingly mischievous! Will you never stop!'

'I suppose I could. It would make a change.'

Light was giving way, but its fate still focused on the Doctor alone. He couldn't maintain this attack for ever: the monster might rally its angry thoughts enough to crush him under its foot like a disconsolate ant. He needed another element now to tip Light's teetering paranoia over the edge. He searched desperately for it and found nothing.

'Nimrod!' pleaded Light in anguish, seeing its confidant watching from the shadows by the lift. 'I can rely on you! Assist me now!'

The manswervant loped slowly towards his god and said, 'I'm sorry, sir. My allegiance is to this planet – my birthright.'

A deep growl rose into a helpless cry of exasperation. 'Everything is changing! All in flux! Nothing remains the same!'

'Even remains decay,' added the Doctor. 'It's this planet. It just can't help itself!'

The data from the ship grated through Light's teeming mind. Its thoughts eluded its grasp; its concentration disintegrated. It defied the corruption with a single, final impulse; it would not be part of this organized chaos called life. 'I . . . will . . . not . . . change! I shall wake up soon!' Its voice was rising into a final feeble whine of despair. 'No . . . change! Dead . . . zero . . .'

It shuddered, twitched and was fixed. An inert, metallic statue stared up at the data that still chattered across the stained-glass screen.

Ace emerged from the drawing room doorway, where she had been watching with Redvers and Control. She clung to the Doctor's arm.

'That's that again, Ace.' The Doctor patted her hand affectionately and looked up at the silent shell of Light's figure. 'Subject for catalogue: file under imagination comma lack of!' There was a bleeped response and he turned to find the others all looking up at the active screen.

Nimrod interceded. 'Excuse me, sir. But Light instigated the firestorm program some time prior to dinner.'

'Ah.'

'What does that mean?' asked Ace.

The Doctor pondered the implication for a split second. 'A very big explosion, very soon.' He started to hurry towards the lift with Ace. With one concerted movement, Control and Redvers, hand in hand, and Nimrod, took their eyes from the data screen and followed.

As the party began their descent in the lift, Josiah, pistol in hand, slipped across the hall. He opened the gates and glared down the shaft at the disappearing lift cage. With a last look back at his house, the master of Gabriel Chase pocketed the gun, adjusted his gloves and swung out onto the descending cable.

The ship emitted its shrill cry as the Doctor led his party through the veil of light. The chamber pulsed with energy as steam jetted from the wall outlets. The two husks were back en tableau in their alcove, standing like waxworks without Control's will to drive the vestigial shreds of life that linked them between her and Josiah. Lozenges of coloured radiance darted through the haze around them, as the crystal rods rose and fell like a steady heart beat or a countdown.

Ace ran straight for the crystal console. 'How do we stop it? Same as before?' she shouted and began to push the rods down into the slab.

'Ace, don't do that!' The Doctor pulled her away from the console.

'It'll nuke Earth!'

'Just look!' He indicated Control, Redvers and Nimrod, who had taken their places in front of one of the ship's data screens. The glow of the patterned alien information flickered across the intent faces.

'Fine time to watch a video!' Ace snapped.

Laying a hand on her shoulder, he asked, 'How does this ship travel?'

'Speed of thought?' she suggested, and then it all snapped into place. 'It's alive!

The Doctor turned slowly in a circle admiring the magnificent stone architechnology. It fermented with living energy right up to its carved inner spire. 'Light's gone, but the ship survives with a new crew.'

Ace didn't see how that would stop the firestorm. An oily, gloved hand caught her round the throat and a gun levelled at her head.

'Turn off the power!' ordered Josiah. 'I'll have my Empire yet!'

Ace struggled and kicked at him. 'Get off me, scumbag!'

'Josiah! Afraid the ship doesn't want you too?' threatened the Doctor.

In their concord of movement, Redvers, Nimrod and Control turned from the screen to face the intruder. Redvers swept his arms out in a magnanimous gesture of friendship. 'There's a place for you here, old chap.' But Josiah held Ace still tighter. He and Control were still linked. She could not leave without him, but neither could he remain on Earth without her. And he would kill to stay. The ship groaned. Control stepped forward, proud and attractive, with a new-found and learned authority. Her jewellery was gone, but a slight sheen on her full skirts threw back the light as they rustled around her.

She threw up a hand and cried, 'Stop! Get back where you belong!'

In the alcove, the head of the reptile husk imploded. Josiah gasped, doubling forward in pain. He collapsed to the floor.

The Doctor caught Ace and they both watched fascinated, as the features of Josiah Samuel Smith lost their colour, melted and reformed, while the creature scrabbled and gurgled in the debris.

157

'There go the rungs on his evolutionary ladder,' observed the Doctor. 'So he falls headlong!'

Ace sneered, 'Go on then, evolve your way out of that one!'

'Poor Control,' croaked the pitiful brute that had been Josiah. 'No way up now. No changing.'

The original Control gently laid her hand on its head and a shower of brittle auburn hair cascaded between her fingers. 'Unhappy creature. I shall look after you.' She slipped a leash over its head and led it away to the cell, where it might stay until she prepared better quarters for it.

'They swapped over,' said Ace, incredulous at the whole balancing act.

'Everyone has their place,' nodded the Doctor. He turned to find that Nimrod was trying to usher them out of the way.

'We have our work to do, sir. Entries and amendments to revise to complete the catalogue.'

'No nukes, then?' said Ace, but Nimrod looked mystified.

'Alice is enquiring as to the explosive potential of the spaceship,' interpreted the Doctor.

Nimrod shook his head. 'No miss, the energy will be redeployed for our departure.' He scurried off on important business. His book of tales would have to wait.

The random gushings of energy and sound had settled into a steadily rising flow. Redvers hurriedly extracted a set of charts from the drawers of the desk. He suddenly understood so much that was new and pondered the holographic patterns of the maps excitedly.

'Redvers has the whole universe to explore for the catalogue! New horizons! Wondrous beasts! Light years out from Zanzibar!'

Control had reappeared and was thumbing through an index file of glowing headings and entries. 'Doctor, somthing tells me you are not in our catalogue.' The Doctor looked awkward and began to sidle towards the tunnel. Control smiled. 'Nor will you ever be,' she reassured him.

The steam began to gush from the outlets again and the new crew took their places before the screens. 'You're busy. Must fly!' called the Doctor. He went to raise his hat, but found he had left it upstairs.

'Bye bye,' called Ace and a chorus of farewells came back through the glowing haze.

'Gone gone,' added the Doctor, hurrying her up into the tunnel. She started to run for the lift.

'Come on! We've got to get clear before the take-off!' she urged as he dawdled behind.

'Take-off?' He nodded backwards. The tunnel ended in solid rock. 'They've gone like a passing thought. As long as their minds don't wander.' He chivvied her into the lift and slammed the doors behind them.

During the ascent, it crossed Ace's mind that the ship's new crew made the weirdest expedition ever. Nimrod would have his work cut out keeping Control and Josiah apart, depending on who was evolutionarily dominant that week. And Redvers would probably want to shoot every new species on sight. Then she remembered the Doctor and herself and decided that as weirdness went, it was probably par for the course.

As they neared the top of the lift shaft, they could hear a loud crackling and rumbling like the violent discharge of electricity.

The hall sank into view, lit by the fierce blue flashes of indoor lightning. Ace had to shield her eyes as they stepped down from the lift, but the Doctor had to look. The shape of Light was still fixed, but there were thin cracks in its shell from which white brilliance seeped. The taut, frozen face of the angel crackled and sparked. Bolts of energy roared out and arced through the house, streaming into the walls and fittings. The flow roared ever faster, until a final eruption of thunder and brilliance which engulfed the whole area. As it faded and the storm rumbled away into the night, the shapes and angles of the house glimmered, picked out in a tracery of phosphorescence. This gradually faded too, but for a while, when Ace blinked, she could see the white shape of Light imprinted on the inside of her eye.

She joined the Doctor and looked at the charred ashen shadow on the tiles where Light had stood. 'It's finally dispersed,' he said and went to fetch his hat and umbrella from the hatstand.

'For ever?' she asked and sat on the stairs. She wanted him to say that the future would be different now, and that a fourteen-year-old delinquent would find a different house in a hundred years' time.

The Doctor noticed that the grandfather clock still said six o'clock. 'The house will remember,' he said. 'Just the ghost of an evil memory lingering. A dark secret after the candle is out.' He reached inside the clock's case and started the pendulum again.

'I felt it here in a hundred years' time.'

'An evil older than time,' he said, making a mental note to avoid certain of the rooms that might upset her on the way back to the TARDIS.

'So I burnt the house down,' she continued.

'Any regrets?'

'Yes.'

'Hmm?'

She grinned. 'I wish I'd blown it up instead.'

That's my girl! thought the Doctor proudly, but he said, 'Wicked!'